Short Stories
with a Cutting Edge

by

Harrison B. Young

Sp

a
Segregansett Imprint

Segregansett Press
P.O. Box 545
Bridgewater, MA 02324-0545

December 1999

ISBN 1-929471-21-1

On the cover: "Chef with Knife." Reworked from an illustration in *Popular Advertising Cuts of the Twenties and Thirties*, edited by Leslie Cabarga. Published as part of the Dover Pictorial Archive Series, 1996. Used with permission.

5 6 7 8 9 10

Published by the *Segregansett Press*, P.O. Box 545, Bridge-water, MA 02324-0545. These stories are fictitious and any resemblance between the characters in them and actual persons is completely coincidental.

Contents

Short Stories with a Cutting Edge

by

Harrison B. Young

A Fine Choice

J ulie and Patrick urgently combed the protection rack at the pharmacy. And people were staring.

"Julie, I really think we should go with the Trojans. I mean after all, that Roman soldier was put there for a reason."

"Eh, I don't know. For my buck, Sheik's the one for the job. I mean they're the most expandable condom on the market today. And you know what a BIG JOB we HAVE." Patrick noticed a woman's face redden behind the lunch counter.

"Great. And now everyone else knows what a big job we have. I have to admit though, their ads are kind of cute."

"Oh, will you forget about the ad quality, Mr. Big Shot on Madison Avenue. We've got to hurry. This is an emergency, remember?" Aghast moans circulated about.

"Excuse me, can I help you 2?" The pharmacist now looked as concerned as they were. "Maybe you'd really like to hurry this up."

"Hey, Julie, look at this brand. Intimates." Patrick picked up the package, as the older boy with the woman behind the lunch counter giggled while the woman tried covering the head of his younger sister against her coat. "I feel good about these. We'll take them." The pharmacist sighed with relief as he rung them up. Sure enough, they contained the leak until the plumber arrived.

The Life
of the Lingerie

It had been a seductive hand-me-down in her family for 5 generations. Her great-great grandmother had worn it initially, back when its power was meant to be kept behind closed doors, and never mentioned.

Then during the Great Depression, it was worn by the daughter of her great-great grandmother in use of a sordid yet successful occupation. For times were tough and money had to be made in any way possible, though it carried little weight through this era.

As the 20th century's greatest conflicts came and went, her grandmother and mother had worn it for the men in their lives who went to do battle with the enemy supreme and keep them safe.

And finally it had been handed down to her, with the premise that she'd only use proper discretion in its wear.

However, still being young and impressionable when she received the gown, she'd decided to wear it after her high school prom, when she'd brought her date home to a sleeping household. Yet as romance turned to lust, she suddenly felt a sense of urgency, a sense that something wasn't quite right.

But the boy was beyond being turned back, his hormones in high gear. Yet to this day, his death remains mysterious, even to her, as the autopsy showed only strap marks from the gown around his neck. But for those who believe in the power of loyalty....

Marathon Runs

Perhaps you've heard of me. I'm an up and coming chef in the new line of culinary artistry. Although I'm 3 quarters French, my cooking tends to take on more of a bohemian style and flavor, as does just about everything about me.

For example, I know for a fact that health and conditioning are primarily spiritual. Which doesn't mean they're not physical as well. What this basically means is, that in order for one to be truly healthy and fit, one must be willing to ingest substances that purify the spirit, so the body can adjust to all phases of nature to envelop it through time and space—therefore enabling it to live long, pure and well.

And MY recipes would purify just about ANYTHING! Like I know how to garnish an artichoke so that all the unsavory feelings of inner spoilage are removed in one fell swoop. It's easy, you just season it with Tabasco, then turn it slowly on the hibachi until it's as crimson as ever. There's a burst of energy that'll get you to move quickly. I can do wonderful things with goat's milk, too. For a real lift, try dunking one of my paprika flavored croutons in a bowl of it, after the goats are fed a strict diet of mangos and olives. Excellent for the nervous system. I feature lots of nuts and prunes in my recipes. But you need to act now if you want my book. Send check or money order to Colon Purge.

Land About Town

D id you ever ask yourself, if you had it all to do over again, would you want to do it differently? And of course, you know the answer's yes, BUT, you realize there's no point in brooding about what you have no control over. SO.

What you do is simply, RATIONALIZE the FOLLOWING: This is my life. I know it sucks NOW. But I'm gettin' there. Slowly but surely, I'm MAKING PROGRESS!

Okay then. Keep telling yourself that. If it makes you feel better, FINE. Or if you THINK it does, then ALL RIGHT. BUT. Just so you know.

I used to be like you. I spent my whole life thinking, it's gonna get BETTER, wait and see. And it HAS. BUT. What "it" is, is NOT what you might think.

You see, the life to which I'm referring, sucked to the VERY END! I never made the big time. Never earned the respect of my fellow human beings. Never even made a NAME for myself. Except LOSER!

And I often wondered during those 70 something years, as I went from being a reclusive, misunderstood child, to a washed up and burnt out blue-collar adult, to a lonely, disrespected senior citizen, whether my independence, which I always DID seem to have going for me, was worth the price of everything else I had not.

Because what was it about being independent I enjoyed which caused me to NOW think, it wasn't really all it was cracked up to be? Was it the way in which I could feel aloof of my fellow human beings—so everyone else's problems would never have to be MY problems—only my delightful reflections, as I was able to laugh at them all, in my own insecurity?

Or perhaps it was the way I always went to the beat of my own drummer, so nobody could ever know of my OWN pain and suffering—only my indifference to them all. As after all, if you were into trying to make them see you hurt, you were weak and fragile, a spineless wimp who deserved no respect, only the agony of the scorn and humiliation of others.

Whereas if you showed indifference and contempt for everyone, you may not have had friends and followers, but at LEAST you were accepted as one who did things one's own way, and

THIS could only be a POSITIVE attribute.

In any case, it's now time for me to be off with my new found flock. I just figured I'd stop in the old neighborhood again in my reincarnated form. So feel free to watch for me and my fellow pigeons blaze trails across the sky, and leave our OWN white trails on your cars and other possessions. Feed us well, okay? You know something, this TEAM stuff is really for the birds!

The
Righteousness Postulate

T he night was made for a good old-fashioned game of charades. Life's little boredoms had settled in quite comfortably with the wind swept ocean waves caressed deliciously on the horizon by a cluster of silver-streaked stars, dancing before the fat, light blue crescent moon like the normal and safe phenomenon of drab.

Now don't get me wrong, it sure beats the harsh alternatives. Hell, I'll take that over drive-by shootings, AIDS contracting acts of unsafe sex and muggings and broken hearts, humiliations and domestic violence both in homes, out of homes and involving homeless, starving people in and out of homes worldwide ANYTIME!

But HEY, I'm a pretty boring FUCK, when you get right down to it. So I guess you could say that sitting here all alone in my cottage on the beach, watching nature do her thing before my eyes and calling it charades, without so much as even a SAFE piece of ass for myself, yet reserved in my fate, and certainly grateful I still have food, electricity and a working television, radio and fairly comfortable bed, I really got nothing to fuckin' complain about, right? Hey, I'll go along with that, since there's no one here to contradict me.

Which must prove my philosophy: I get what I deserve— i.e. I'm good enough to survive but not to live, leaving me to wonder but one thing—is the view as GOOD in the mountains, tonight?

The
Power
of the Voice

Young love. Confidence. Power. All 3 go together when it involves 2 people who have it going on with each other. Plethoras of experience which include either phasing out the rest of the world, or manipulating it for the benefit of the relationship.

Perhaps showing off arm in arm — and letting the geeks of the world know what they're missing — as if much of the satisfaction which comes with being a young, attractive couple is letting them SEE what they DON'T, and will NEVER have. It must be a wonderful feeling; like the delight which comes from pretending he and she are someone ELSE while you're DOING it, but knowing that I'VE got the BEST and NOBODY could EVER take the place of YOU!

Of course, at THIS point, they might need a little help. HEY! You don't ever need to feel ashamed of needing a little help, when you're in LOVE! Of course, it's merely therapeutic — NOT the cheating kind of help which could permanently fuck up the values of such a wonderful commitment — no sir!, no ma'am! — the empire must remain STRONG and STURDY! So at THIS point, perhaps it's the right time for some counseling, or shopping for a textbook on HOW to keep it together, when the lust for that special one has now become...well, how would you say? — perhaps just a tad FLIMSY?

After all, you're not high school sweethearts anymore; uh, uh, you're BEYOND that NOW — time to think about the NEXT step.

So then you 2 decide to become analytical — HOWEVER — therein lies the REAL problem; because for either one of you to readily admit to the other, that your genitalia is feeling a longing for ANYONE outside the realm of OUR relationship, would be lover's suicide. THEREFORE, this problem must be approached with care and delicacy — so NOW what the fuck happened to HONESTY, HMM?

And in finally figuring out together on a MUTUAL basis how to deal with this problem, WITHOUT disclosing either one's PERSONAL desires, you guys ultimately reach a solution to the problem at hand — as up to NOW, the ONLY revelation you've each made to the other, is how you both feel the need to COMMUNICATE better in the relationship — and after all, this could ONLY mean the PEAK of innocence for BOTH of you! Hey, no ideas of cheating here. Or here either.

So what you 2 have now decided to do is take a seminar on the science of perfecting one's ELOQUENCE together — something truly designed JUST for you. This way, you'll EACH be able to feel more CONFIDENT and POWERFUL (and POWER-FUL really IS the KEY word in THIS case) in talking together. And since you've both agreed to do this, there can be NO friction or resentment between you after all is said and done. You're simply going to learn how to really talk things out — just what's so for the sake of CUPID'S ARROW.

It's a bit expensive, but you both know it's worth every dig, for the price of love can ONLY be measured once it's lost.

So enthusiasm soon begets participation, as you both sit in the giant-sized room at the Hilton in town, and take in all the rhetoric and instructions of the speaker. "When you need to make a point, you must send a message loud and clear," he chants, and then quickly bellows where he feels it's necessary, "like when I say to you, how can you TREAT ME this way?" His eyes have become wild and fiery, his fists and jaw are clenched with directness. The audience recoils in their reaction, and you're both extremely impressed. "There you see," he continues, "I haven't made my partner feel GUILTY, I've just been DIRECT and HONEST. And my message is transmitted in such a way that my partner feels like, 'Hey, I GOT it!' And then of course, it's my PARTNER'S turn to respond in kind. THUS, the art of communication is perfected, AND the relationship is STRENGTHENED. Now come on. Any volunteers?"

Naturally you both go first. And as the seminar continues you perfect the technique. And when you finally go home, you're set. The next few weeks go by and you each get better and better. And then one day, during a small argument, you both begin to weaken. Then you're UNCOMFORTABLE together. Before you know it, you're cowering in separate corners, wishing there was a next step.

Caricature of a Rainbow

G ive me some of the reddest damn wine — right
from the vine of an abused and splattered
grape; so life's true bloodletting may finally begin.
The feeling of conquest shall be exquisite and
everlasting, as if fortresses of state which have stood
for eons have at last collapsed under the fierce
weight of pressure put upon them by the soldiers of
destiny who were once lowly peasants until such
time as their calling to duty carried them on a pious
mission of glory. The crown of nobility shall now
reign supreme over that of purposelessness, as every
sea with billions upon billions of spiraling waves
shall be forever stilled — caught in a brilliant frozen
collage of blue and white ice, each colored edge
finally neutralized before the other — as the humility
of battle has ended in a fixated mass to be admired
and critiqued with no count or score kept, as the
finiteness of the universe is now put to rest.

Nature's greens and browns are bombed beyond
recognition — the semblance of still beauty reflected
in them along with massive portions of mixed in
black and grey — the only evidence of any formerly
moving and destructive life. And in the final swirl
of a stilled world, we celebrate in our souls, the
knowledge of how it all ended — the supreme artist's
abstract spills upon a canvas of nothingness — to no
end sacrificed for the wile of eternity.

Dust Buster

In the 500th century A.D., after several thousand changes in evolution had occurred following 3 ice ages, 2 major nuclear confrontations and many large scale laser battles, survival had become the most important subject among earth's more intelligent inhabitants. Due to the unalterable infertility that had affected all but a few billion tiny amoeba dwellings as a consequence of mutation, nature's ecosystems were deteriorating rapidly. The greatest minds available to find other resources for the planet's recovery had gathered around the transparent Holy Dome at Oracle Square. Inkerstel, High Priest of the Zandas, earth's most advanced race, and his brethren were aligned about in a circle with their tentacles locked tightly together.

The greenish-gray of the early evening sky over the decaying parapets around Oracle Square was filled with a cold somberness. The Zandas were in prayer for their lives. Outside the parapets, ever smaller groups of star birds provided minimal nourishment for sparse and sickly clamp vines, which once through healthy photosynthesis had kept the Zandas thriving.

It was their last hope, but they lost no faith. History's most significant miracles had occurred at this sacred site, including the Dome's formation. More cosmic energy had been released through the Dome than anywhere else, and it was figured the

Gods had erected it for the purpose of exchanges with the Chosen One. Inkerstel now lifted his receptor as high above the Dome as he could, where he sensed a stream of energy was pushing its way straight up through the center. Then for the first time since the Final Conflict, the earth trembled violently and Inkerstel slid his crustaceous body up onto the Dome, while the brethren chanted loudly. The message was as clear as it had been since Inkerstel learned here he was the Chosen One, and bits and pieces of knowledge from an extinct world pierced his soul to help him guide the Zandas away from their own destruction.

He knew the world would be saved after all, and no sacrifice was too great for the purpose. As the ground blew open in front of them, the brethren maintained their tentacle lock until the Dome and Inkerstel shattered into many fragments and vanished. The crystal substance that filled the sky was amazingly beautiful. The brethren exclaimed to each other telepathically that neither Inkerstel or the Dome could ever be replaced, and they would be eternally grateful to both. The dust continued to swirl about in the sky and spin out toward the horizon, and soon touched everything living on the planet.

Before long life forms began to thrive again with the humus that was trapped in the earth for eons once again nourishing land and sea. For the Zandas, and much of the world population which was also telepathic, cosmic energy from the dust created images of life as it used to be: of creativity, love, hate, disease, natural disaster and the need for power. But what was mostly implied in the telepathic messages was life could really be wonderful if precautions were taken to guard against ruinous mistakes. When the knack for creativity began to affect the Zandas after a few generations, a shrine was erected in Oracle Square, where the Dome had been—of Inkerstel on the Dome.

It came to be the symbol of the Holy Savior, and eventually bequeathed the start of a new religion which survived both time and the elements. It was worshipped for centuries, until amoebas cross bred with sea weed led to the growth of a fatal fungi that wiped out the Zandas as well as most of the land's population, but the shrine still stood unscathed.

As evolution dwindled on land, it thrived again on the ocean floor when many spores from the fungi hatched tail finned amoebas that preyed on their ancestors. More elongated creatures were generated until one day an offspring slithered up on land and found a mate. After awhile, hair, hands and feet began to appear.

The Triangle

In case anyone ever tells you to follow your heart, instead of your brain, remind them of which of those irreplaceable parts CAN'T outlast the other. Then explain to them why logic is NOT a dead science. At least not quite yet.

What I wouldn't give now to have had someone sit me down a few weeks ago and hand me that lecture. I may have had trouble buying it, but you'd better believe, there have been many successful arguments for its application— "Look at that Titanic baby; she's a beauty; why COULDN'T she survive a 3 ton glacier? What do you mean, Louis, treat the peasants like humans? Let 'em eat CAKE, I say! Hey, Chris! Before you go sailing, don't you think you'd at LEAST better attach those boats to something with a rope?" Well, you get the idea. And oh, by the way, if you feel impatient for the gist of this story, I'm not surprised. Whoever said patience is a virtue was obviously as stupid as I was about 3 weeks ago.

ANYWAY! It all began...well, technically it began during my youth when I somehow managed to overdevelop my rambunctiousness and under-develop my communication skills, i.e., I wanted an EASY answer for everything. BUT! This particular problem began later, as I waited tables at a small quaint café on the boardwalk, known as—get this— a small quaint café on the boardwalk.

Now before I go on, and brace yourself—you may be seeing a LOT of that in this narrative before I'm through—after all, only someone as quirky as I am could create a piece of fiction like this and I need a few fillers just for getting my OWN rocks off, BUT, I just want to make it crystal clear, this ain't no fable, cause I don't DO fables, BUT, I'll STILL try to keep the tale mercifully short for you, in spite of all the nonsense.

Ever briefly though, just let me explain what separates this kind of piece from an actual fable. In an actual fable, there's a moral of some kind, usually of virtue and/or nobility, yet in THIS case scenario, the only alternative to the outcome I've HAD to experience is to either pay STRICT attention to who drinks the love potion, or not even BOTHER with the fuckin' potion, which as it turned out I really didn't NEED to—well—what do you know? Maybe this story really IS a fable, after all!

ANYWAY! Time is growing short now, and I must move on before it's too late, yes that's right, I have a deadline, assuming I'm really living this tale, and HE'S out there, sniffing ME out. And I really don't want to be here and have him find me—for WOE is me if he does, so I'd better just proceed with the fuckin' story as quick as I can—before he gets here and has his way with me, in which case I'll then have ANOTHER story I don't WANT to have.

Okay, then, just so you know, I stand about 5,6,

and weigh roughly 138. What does that have to do with this story, you ask. By itself, nothing. But combine that with the fact that I'm a shy lad from Passaic, with an inferiority complex, and a tendency to drink bicarbonate of soda whenever I get nervous — being under the impression it will solve my gas problem — which often happens when I'm REALLY nervous, and you have 1/3 of the scenario.

The other 2/3rds are Diane, who was a regular customer at a small quaint café on the boardwalk, remember that place where I waited tables? Her BOSS, one Belvedere Davis, an Australian body builder who stands about 6,7, and weighs some 275 lbs., of which a good, and the term "good," in THIS case I DO use loosely, but anyway, before I lose YOUR train of thought, his percentage of body fat on that frame is in a BAD range of about 8%. And what I DIDN'T know as I waited on their table, every afternoon at lunch time, was that Diane actually DETESTED Belvedere! I THOUGHT they were an ITEM, being they were always together, AND being that HE was always on her like white on rice, ham and rye, tuna in casserole, well, enough with the food analogies, those were usually the daily specials at a small quaint café on the boardwalk I needed to memorize as a waiter. And being I was a pretty good one, I guess they kind of stuck in my head. ANYWAY!

I'm not really sure what business they were in, I think it may have been some kind of vitamin sales.

And that was ONLY based on the way both Diane
and Belvedere LOOKED. There's never been any
actual disclosure in the letters she sent me.

YES, that's right. SHE—small, firm, petite, legs
to die for, butter-smooth hair and cheeks—sends
letters to ME. Letters of, well, I suppose you could
call it SINCEREST remorse COMBINED with "if
ONLY we HADN'T been so HASTY and IMPUL-
SIVE!" Because THEN, we'd BOTH be set RIGHT, as
in TOGETHER, and that creep Belvedere would
be in JAIL where he belongs, or at the very LEAST,
in the throes of a sexual harassment suit bigger than
his fuckin' biceps and pecs COMBINED!

But unfortunately—as in many cases where
communication is bypassed for assumption—we DID
act impulsively. AND! As from the WAY we acted
as such, came our FIRST indication to the OTHER,
how we really DID have something in common.
Something we were able to detect with our own
EYES, and NOT have to find out AFTER it was too
late, by desperate mail correspondence to a diverse
assortment of mobile locations—at least mobile in
MY case, as I dare NOT stay in one place very long,
out of fear HE may find me. And that particular item
which, as it turned out, we'd actually noticed about
each other simultaneously was our NEWSPAPER,
A.C.U.

Now for you NORMAL people, for lack of
a BETTER word—since who the hell is REALLY
normal—that's Atlantic City Underground.   And

believe you me, the kind of stuff you can find in THIS paper really IS underground. LITERALLY! That's why I didn't find it too shocking that the location of one Doctor Durango, a remedial ace from some island very few this side of the equator have heard of, was right below the subway station in Trenton. Nor did Diane find it too surprising.

What I DID find MOST surprising, was how on that afternoon a few weeks back, when I happened to be reading A.C.U. during my break, and looked briefly over at Diane with that HUNKAMUNK beside her, who ALSO happened to be reading it, how BOTH our eyes caught the same ad, simultaneously. AND! How BOTH our INTENTIONS were the SAME. Oh, by the way, just so you know, THIS was the ad: In case the throb of your heart neither knows nor cares that you're alive, stop in for a dose of Durango Mango. For the PERMANENT affection of that special one.

Well, to continue to make a short story much LONGER than it probably NEEDS to be, that's what both Diane and myself ended up doing. In fact, we probably just missed each other at his office by MOMENTS. But I would've been so tongue-tied, and fearful of BELVEDERE, it probably wouldn't have mattered even if we hadn't!

ANYWAY! This, as it turned out, is what happened NEXT. She had a plan. I had a plan. HER plan was to slip the potion into MY bicarbonate of soda which I ALWAYS kept on the tray with me while I served them. MY plan was simply to slip the potion into HER glass of Perrier which she had everyday with lunch.

Unfortunately, on the day of this fiasco, and BELIEVE you ME, it was NOTHING short of one, although I really DO think that's putting it MILDLY, either SHE ended up putting the potion in BEL-VEDERE'S drink instead of mine, in an attempt to be covert, as I had my back turned to THEM, OR, I ended up putting it in HIS drink by mistake, as I was so fuckin' NERVOUS!

ANYWAY! (for the KAZILLIONTH fuckin' time) That part of the story DOESN'T matter. What DOES matter, is what Belvedere said to ME, when I came back with their check. "Ho aah ya, mate, caya ti cyum dayiwn undir weth may?"

Suffice it to say, I bolted from there like a skinny dipper from a piranha pit. But that hasn't mattered to Belvedere. He's really a slick one. When I started seeing him at my windows after receiving Diane's first letter, I knew I had to be out of there. Since she gave me HER address, I'm able to keep in touch from the tiny motels I've been staying at. Someday, maybe I'll find an antidote. Or maybe HE'LL die from a steroid overdose! SEE YA.

Tyrone

M e and Tyrone have been the best of friends now for almost 20 years. He's been as loyal as a fired-up engine to a drag racer. And I've been as good to him as his teat hangin' old bitch mama, before the canine angel at the Pearly Gates called her home.

Yup. Me and old Ty, we seen hell and high water together. As a pup, he brought me more joy when he bit that Jehovah's Witness than my poor old late wife, Myrtle, brought me when she accepted my marriage proposal. It was as if somebody up there had finally decided to send me down a companion who even thought like me.

But old Ty, he's got his sentimental side as well. When he saw those 2 humungus raccoons trying to make a snack of my trash, he took it upon himself to ever so neatly bring them some of the leftover meat scraps I put out on his plate for him. Yup. I love old Ty. And so did the raccoons after that.

Sometimes Myrtle would even say she felt I cared more for that big stupid dog than her. And that wasn't true at all. It's just that he was always so helpful to me and independent-like, where Myrtle needed me for just about every dagnabbin' thing there was. I hunted, fished, shopped and cooked. All with the help of Tyrone. And all Myrtle ever did was mope around in that squeaky old wheelchair of hers. And what I found MOST amusing was how

Tyrone would promptly break wind every time
Myrtle complained.

And what's more, the LAST thing Tyrone is is
stupid! It seems to me, Myrtle was the one who was
so out of it, she couldn't even find her way around
the house without tripping over something. That's
why she spent her final years in a wheelchair—she
was so bruised from falling all the time—like she
could never get USED to the way Tyrone always
moved the furniture for MY convenience.

Yup, that's right. Ever since I've had him,
Tyrone's been my personal mover/interior deco-
rator. Many dogs bring people their slippers. Ty's
always known how to push ottomans, chairs, tables
and the television set. And it's as if he's always
known how much I love variety, and Myrtle could
never quite get used to this.

Unfortunately, one day out in the yard, old Ty
happened to push Myrtle a little too close to our well
after she'd dozed off. She'd had cotton in her ears,
as his barking had been too loud for her. I KNOW
he just wanted her to have peace and quiet. But the
rest—as they say—was tragic history, as Myrtle who
was leaning right over it went straight down and
either drowned or broke her neck. I don't think she
suffered much, praise the Lord.

Of course, both me and Ty were devastated, but
accidents DO happen, right, boy? And he knows I'll
always worship the ground he walks on, no matter
how lonely it gets around here. And someday, all

this will be HIS. And I couldn't think of ANYONE more deserving of my small but comfortable fortune than old Ty!

Yes, sir. He's been so helpful to my more personal needs too.

For example. I'm a diabetic, and I have to take insulin every day. And Ty, who's so self-sufficient, he can actually take his own meals from the pantry and water from the well, can ALSO bring me my insulin. And he's been doing so for many years.

Now the fact that the insulin may have been diluted for some time, which the doctors attribute to my current blindness, has prompted me to file a lawsuit against the drugstore. But with the legal process being so slow and bogged down, I doubt I'll even live long enough to see one dime of my settlement. But I'm sure old Ty here will do just fine with it when it comes in, won't you, boy?

He sure is a great old pal. I wonder where he's taking me today. I hear the noise of the city all around. It seems we've been walking for miles. But what the hey, he knows how much I love to walk, don't you, boy? Of course, I don't think we've ever gone THIS far. Oh, well. Boys will be boys and dogs will be dogs. They ALL love to explore new horizons. What's this? Hey, we're stopping. He's pulling me down. He wants me to lie down. Okay. I guess I am a little tired. Must be a picnic in the park. I hear lots of traffic. Sure I'll take a nap with you, you big lug!

Floatation Failure

The S.S. Chrysanthemum was boarded for the long cruise to the Caribbean. Among the passengers were several couples, some out to relive the magic of their matrimony, with others out just to try to rekindle it. The Captain welcomed everyone as he stood by with his broad shoulders straight and postured and an easy smile, while the crew copied his proper stance as they were lined up in an orderly formation.

This wasn't the type of cruise people ever took lightly—the cost alone was staggering. The perks included a month of the most luxurious meals and accommodations provided to anyone in the free world. Of course, like everything else in life, the bottom line was whether or not they could make their own fun aboard the vessel. And in the last few years, there had actually been major changes in the statuses of many lives of passengers who'd boarded for their cruise of a lifetime. And hopefully this time, none of them would be for the worse.

"Well, Stanley, are you ready to be wiped out in a game of shuffleboard?" Flora Kessler asked her husband, after they'd seen their living quarters for the next 4 weeks. "I think your ego could use a little taming, after the way those accounts you just picked up really went to your brain!" Stanley Kessler was not a man who took being outdone lightly, but thrived on competition.

"Really, Flora. I thought we were on this cruise to relax and unwind. But there's never a dull moment with you, is there?"

"And I aim to keep it that way. Because dull is always the prerequisite to disaster. Just look at some of the other couples that are on the boat with us. I can see desperate written all over their faces!"

"Oh, and we're so much better off, is that what you're trying to tell me? We still can't seem to just be alone together, without having some kind of friction!"

"Exactly. That's why I think a little friendly shuffleboard competition will do us a lot of good. It'll relieve the tension. And give us the chance to work on our tans at the same time."

"All right, then. So why do you have to say you're going to kick my ass? Why can't you just say, let's have a friendly game of shuffleboard? Everything with you, Flora, is about trying to top someone!"

"Well, you're a fine one to talk. Look at you in business!"

"That's different, and you know it. It's a dog-eat-dog world out there. And it's a good thing I'm as aggressive as I am! Just where do you think you'd be today if I wasn't?"

Flora knew it was best to let it go at this. There'd be no point in getting in over her head. "Okay, then. Shuffleboard?"

The Mabelsons were in the lounge, taking

advantage of the all you can eat buffet. Maurice filled his plate with a dozen crab cakes, and in whatever space was left he scooped in as much shrimp as it could hold without spilling over. "Don't you think that's a bit much?" asked his wife, Gertie, as she doused the 20 or so lobster claws on her own plate with enough butter from the dispenser to make it look like they'd been drowned in urine.

"Are you going to give me nothing but a hard time for these next 4 weeks? I swear, I knew this was a bad idea!"

"All right, I'm sorry. It's just that I know how much you're going to complain about the cost of all this. And seeing you eat like this just reinforces your argument about wasteful spending!"

"Oh, you're a fine one to talk, Miss Swim-in-Lobster-Piss!"

"Maurice! Please watch your mouth. This is supposed to be a classy cruise. And all I meant was that after all this is over I know you're probably going to be upset about the cost, if you don't have a great time."

"Fine! Well then why don't you just shut up so I can have a great time!"

Now ready to indulge for the first time since they'd boarded, the Mabelsons sat down in a quilted booth and began to dig in. After awhile, a waitress asked if everything was okay. "Um, bum, mum," they said, butter and scraps dripping all over.

The Bachmans were in the casino, trying to

decide between roulette or blackjack. "Look, Effie, there's a system to winning at blackjack, where roulette is sheer, odds staggering chance."

"But playing roulette is so much more distinguished, where blackjack reminds me of gangsters."

"What the hell are you talking about, Effie?"

"What do you mean, what am I talking about? You know very well what I'm talking about, George. All the speakeasies of the roaring '20s had blackjack. All the gambling casinos run by the mob have blackjack. People get rubbed out if they win at blackjack in the wrong circles!" He gave her his typical "you're an idiot" look.

"Well, in case you hadn't noticed, you shmagegi, we're on a CRUISE ship now!" He took her shoulders and slowly shook her to make his point. "There are NO, GANGSTERS, ANYWHERE, ON, THIS, BOAT, HELLO!"

Upstairs on deck, the Captain was scouting around, not only to see if the passengers were comfortable, but also to make SURE, nothing was going on which could mean disaster for their love lives, as an assortment of sordid events which had occurred involving passengers on previous cruises had done in years past.

At the moment, everything seemed okay. But considering this was only the first day of the cruise, Captain Maguire knew from experience that keeping guard duty on everyone would have to just about be a full-time job. After all, it wasn't until the middle of the second week of his first cruise, he found out about how an older man, who was supposed to be on his second honeymoon, which their CHILDREN had bought them no less, had seduced a young woman in her cabin, while her newlywed husband was trying to have his way with one of the matrons in the lounge. Apparently, those 2 married too young, and suffice it to say, it led to quite a cat fight between the young female newlywed and the older man's wife. Not to mention an escalation of more such events, as well as the threats of lawsuits which never amounted to anything, as nobody could prove negligence or malice on the part of the cruise line. But this was definitely the kind of stuff which had caused them to jack up the price of the cruise considerably, in order to make sure only the most exclusive individuals got on board.

And now Captain Maguire passed a young man who was also a newlywed, whose in-laws owned a Texas oil refinery. "Wha, hey, Cayaptain Magwya? Yi ba ana chayance seyen ma Maydeline?"

"No, Billy-Joe, I haven't. Maybe she's back in your cabin."

This couldn't be hanky-panky — it was too scandal risky.

"Weyell, awl riyat. Shay wayas juyust meovin' suhm foldeen chayas. I prawbly shyould've beeyin hyelpin' hyer. Thank yi, syo kindlay, seer."

Captain Maguire gave him a reassuring smile.

"Anytime, Billy-Joe. Remember, if you need anything at all, you know where I am." Better they come to him, then him to them.

"Thank yi agayan, syo kindlay, seer."

They each went their separate ways, both fairly confident everything was okay. And now that Captain Maguire had pretty much scanned the whole ship, and things seemed under control with the passengers for the moment, it was time to check in with his crew and see how everything was going from their end.

He proceeded down to the navigation room first, to take a look at the autopilot. Everything was running smoothly, and the ship was traveling straight, calm and slow. Randy, his first mate was now out of the room, but Captain Maguire knew how reliable he was, and how boring it could be, watching and listening to the hum of a motorized compass, especially when there were other things that needed checking from time to time.

Now content all was well on the navigational front, Captain Maguire headed to the lounge for a plate of shrimp cocktail and to relax a bit. Wouldn't it be a miracle if this cruise actually turned out to be the best one he'd ever been able to head up.

But it was when he passed by the servants' quarters on his way to the lounge, he heard the shocking moans. No way, how could this be happening? But it was. And what made it all the worse, was THIS time, it was Randy. His first mate. His

trusted and loyal sea partner for the past 5 years.
And he knew from the sound of the woman, it had
to be Maydeline Jenkins. No way! Poor Billy-Joe! It
would KILL him!

Captain Maguire knew he had to keep his wits
about him. But what could he do, what would he say
to Randy? It was like he needed some kind of a
miracle — some way to tell Randy he was no longer
his right-hand man, without letting anything get
beyond this portal. Otherwise, the scandal and pain
to result would be nothing short of total devastation.

Obviously, there was no way he could stop to
eat now. Nor could he interrupt them, or wait for
them to finish, like the scoutmaster of his most
honorable troop awaiting the arrival of his number
one cub, only to let him know there was no longer
any place for him in the scouts.

So after a few minutes of thought, Captain
Maguire decided to return to the navigation room,
where he expected Randy would join him shortly.
And then he'd simply have to handle the matter as
delicately as he could. This had to be the biggest
catch-22 ever.

However, on his way back to the navigation
room, he heard the other sounds. The ever growing
noise of loud commotions starting to occur all over
the ship. The thuds of shuffleboard equipment
thrashing about in all directions, gave way to much
screaming and swearing from up there. Then the
horrific thwaks and yells of a food fight now

escalating in the lounge, which had begun to include some of the personnel, as well as most of the unruly patrons. This was also complemented by the thrashing of metal tokens all about the casino, which resulted in what looked like a giant slot machine had just delivered a major jackpot all over Fort Knox. In any case, the pandemonium now erupting had caused Captain Maguire to rethink his entire strategy in a hurry.

After running to his private quarters as fast as he could, he turned on the intercom and made the following announcement. "The cruise has now been canceled due to the emergency in progress. If everyone would quickly calm down and cooperate, full refunds will be given to each passenger, once we return to port. If not, then I'll simply leave this vessel through my secret compartment and you're all free to fend for yourselves. Thank you. And it's been a pleasure serving you." Captain Maguire's announcement quickly brought the crisis and his long and proud career to a grand and memorable finish. The S.S. Chrysanthemum would sail no more.

Play Safely

Hebshie the Irish Setter was outside, howling like a wolf. It was if all the fun they'd ever had together over the years had finally reached the PEAK of its negative impact stage—like a great dream now gone completely amiss, with only the most awful of consequences to follow their terribly mislaid plans. Of course, this WAS a most special night, and Marla knew that in only a matter of about 45 minutes or so, she'd TRULY be able to start her life over.

"Hey, mom, is the moon really that full tonight?" asked Toby, as he casually meandered into the living room, where Marla lay on the sofa in a near state of undress with Dan. She quickly flopped the hem of her robe down to her feet, as Dan zipped his fly up, and they both sat up.

"What the hell are you doing out of bed?" she demanded. "I thought I said we wanted to be alone. Doesn't that mean ANYTHING to you?"

"But how can I sleep with Hebshie making all that noise?" Toby seemed quite oblivious to what was going on between his mother and Dan, which was mostly due to his weaning.

"The kid's right," Dan added, almost humorously. "I'll be honest with you Marla, I was having a hard time concentrating myself."

Marla now wondered if the world was ganging up on her. "You know something, I need a drink," she said, standing up in exasperation and guilt. "Why can't anything ever go RIGHT, anymore?"

Dan stomped his feet on the floor as she left the room for the liquor cabinet. "Damn floozy lush," he muttered, almost in spite of the fact that her son was now giving him his typical, aren't you going to be my new daddy kind of look.

Hebshie continued howling away, and got louder and louder as the moment grew nearer. Of course, Marla knew the Jack Daniels would soon drown that out — the way it would drown out everything else. Or at the very LEAST, it might make this seem more like Halloween, and not the MOURNING cry of an old grieving dog, who somehow KNEW the best friend he ever had was about to be a goner.

Marla tried to forget how the 3 of them used to be such a great team. Oh, sure, Buddy would sometimes beat both of them. Of course, it was only SHE he'd ever smack to a pulp — Hebshie he'd only whack with a stick from time to time. And that was just for his own good he'd tell him — to keep him from doing anything stupid, like digging through contaminated trash, or trespassing on property where he might be shot. And apparently it worked, because not ONLY was Hebshie one of the most well-behaved dogs, he was also extremely loyal. Which is why he'd turned on Marla.

Over at the prison, last minute preparations were being made to sizzle Buddy. The guard shaved his head and chest down to a bare pulp. It seemed as if this was the neatest he'd ever looked.

But he wasn't scared to die. If anything it would be the best alternative. Living in a world of people who'd betrayed him from day one—broken home, parents he never knew past the age of 5, brothers and sisters who stole from him left and right, then an orphanage run by nuns who always slapped him silly, degraded him verbally, and washed his mouth out with Boraxo any time he spoke out of turn—dying made that other stuff seem like a fuckin' picnic.

So was it any wonder he'd taken to a life of crime? And just when he thought he'd found someone who really cared about and understood him—someone who had a very similar background, yet with a little more spending cash to begin with, to help him open a small diner, and teach him how to cook short-order, but when the bucks stopped rolling in, and times got a little tough for their business, she takes HIM hostage, forces him to rob a fuckin' convenience store, and wouldn't you know it, because HE'D had a criminal record dating back to the nunnery with a car theft, a few unarmed robberies and a violent assault, they pin the murder on HIM, even though SHE pulled the damn trigger. Marla, you CUNT! Plus HE grabbed for the gun, so they connected his fingerprints.

If only Hebshie talked. He was the only living witness to the crime. And that sick broad thought it was a big kick to bring him along. That was mostly what he had to live for now. Hebshie had always been completely loyal to him. If only there was some way Buddy could let him know how he felt about him.

Of course he got Marla pregnant just before she lost it. He was already in here by the time she had him — what had she named the kid? Something like Hobey or Robey. But what difference did it make. He wouldn't know the kid today if he tripped over him.

And now the guard was here to take Buddy for his last walk. The chaplain stood beside him and read out of the big black book. Buddy actually found it kind of relaxing.

"The Lord is my Shepherd, I shall not want... ashes to ashes, dust to...though I walk through the valley of the shadow of...shall fear no evil...my Lord in Heaven." When they arrived Buddy casually sat down and got himself comfortable.

Each strap was adjusted but not the hood. "Is there anything at all you'd like to say, or something we can do for you, Mr. Mackenzie?" The warden appeared stern yet sympathetic.

"Gee, warden, could you get my hopes up a little higher?"

With the hood placed, the switch was pulled, and smoke and soil purged from Buddy Mackenzie — his horrific scream a silent hell.

Toby had frantically gone outside. Hebshie had

just run off, and he'd no idea what to do. Of course, Dan was already long gone, as was his patience with Marla. "Where are you, Hebshie? Please come on home now!"

After he'd run back and forth along the street for 5 minutes, Toby decided to get Marla. But he found by then she was passed out drunk on the kitchen floor.

"Please, mom, not NOW! Wake up, get up. Hebshie ran away!" But she just continued to lie there, forgetful of what she'd accomplished. Buddy was dead, as a result of HER actions. She'd committed the perfect crime, and now she'd be getting a sweet little chunk from his life insurance company. With some luck, it might be enough to supplement the bills after using up most of her welfare checks on booze and trampy clothing to attract ever more of the same kind of men she always had. Violent predators who took no interest in her or Toby, only what they could get for themselves. Of course, she HAD been thinking about buying back the diner, but chances were she wouldn't have enough even with what she had coming. But what mattered most was simply avoiding trouble. Sooner or later, she'd wake up, Toby would come to terms with his beloved pet being too distraught to ever return, and life would go on. How could things be better? How indeed.

The Face of Danger

Traffic continued to buzz by at a nearly alarming rate. While the street was where it belonged, there were times it seemed like the grim reaper was just waiting to pounce down, like a cat in the dimension of erewhon suddenly seizing its prey without any clue to its prior whereabouts.

Of course, Ben had it under control—or so it seemed—as if the hours between 2 and 3 every afternoon on school days were his final calling. The decorated policeman had done lots of hard time on the force, with this the slice of heaven a retirement pension for capturing dangerous criminals over 40 years couldn't match.

He'd had many chances for a desk job during his career, with higher pay and more perks. But when it came right down to it, Ben knew he belonged out there bagging the criminal element, and even getting shot a few times (once to the point of being in a nearly fatal coma for 3 days) couldn't keep him inside the station. Of course, he was more than happy with the pay increase.

But now the children were what mattered most. He'd never had any—the career man whose liability in life was way too risky to ever start a family he might've suddenly had to be taken from forever. And this was what brought him joy in the twilight of his grand profession—being out here with these young, innocent children—sending them on their way, smiling and safe.

"Hi, Benny," they'd say to him each day as he held up the traffic for them with his stocky arms, still ripe with muscles after 65 years. It still always seemed like the challenges which went with the job were ever-present, as if the power he had to stop all those impatient motorists to gain the children's trust and love was just as exciting as when the risk and danger of his occupation was at its peak.

"Hi there, boys and girls," he'd say as they all anxiously approached the crosswalk, with him looking like he was trying to wave to them, without inadvertently giving the go-ahead signal to the drivers.

"Did everyone have a nice day in school?"

They'd always give him a wide range of answers, which sounded much like the eager responses they might give to a children's TV show host, were they lucky enough to appear on a live broadcast. In any case, Ben knew that their seeing him at the end of the school day—their final liaison to the freedom of the outside world, was what made the afternoon complete for each of them. Or so it seemed.

And this was truly what Ben lived for now. To get to feel like the sentimentalist he seemed was the best break he ever had. After all, what better way to put his final jewel in the crown.

He'd finally decided to make the move today. Of course, he'd thought long and hard while he planned it out. It wasn't an easy choice, but from rationalizing for many weeks now, Ben felt that after all his years of unwavering dedication to the force, he truly deserved it in no uncertain terms.

He realized it was something everyone would frown upon if they knew, yet in his heart, Ben felt he was just one more person seeking out what God had intended for him. And if done discreetly and with conviction, then the true love he had inside himself would indeed prevail over the normal stereotype he'd had to live under his entire life as to enable him to reach this point of the highest enlightenment.

He continued to smile at the children as they crossed. If the late ones were okay with donuts, it should be a breeze. These were usually the troublemakers anyway—the ones who were kept after school for disrupting, bullying; all the stuff that Ben could help straighten out while he gave them his undivided, quite intimate and most private kind of attention.

At this point, he'd lost all his inhibitions and continued to watch and wait. But in his absent-mindedness, he drifted back out into the street and was squashed like a bug, leaving everyone in the community to cope with the much lesser of 2 tragic evils.

Freeze Boy

The line was long and restless. All walks of life filled the aisle. Musical aspirations were never stronger as sudden gigs had begun to break out among the groups. "I'll be seein' you honey, before too long. I've come this far, so we gotta know it can't be wrong," sang the 5 young men who called themselves the Torches, using a do-op rhythm similar to a '50s glee club. "Oh, BABY, let ME be the one," added the Harmonettes, a sextet of sleek women in miniskirts and low-cut blouses. The James Gang, a biker-type group with 3 big bearded guys and 3 punky gals, all clad in tight black leather jackets appeared to be the most intimidating of the bunch. 2 of the guys played guitars which looked as used as a Harley with 50,000 miles, while the other one fingered a portable keyboard. The 3 girls accompanied them on drums and cymbals in a way reminiscent of the music played in a loud, rowdy bar.

Amazingly, because of the way the room was structured, no one sound completely drowned out any of the others. Derek had made sure of this when he built the studio. There was no point in constructing a waiting room where all the talents vying for his attention would have to resent each other any more than they had to. There'd be enough resentment after he'd made his selections, since the competition had worked so hard to get THIS far, and only SO many could be good enough to get a deal with his company.

Derek was watching them perform from the one-way window in his soundproof office. Before he made any selections he wanted to study them carefully. He could tell a great deal by seeing their moves before he heard them, and in his 12 years in the business, he'd never been wrong about the success of his picks.

Of course, he still had to make the right picks, and he had to do it before any of them got too frustrated. And he knew what sounded great and would sell, and what didn't and wouldn't. So it was now time to call each group in and listen for what lay ahead.

The sound room was right off the waiting room. Derek would call over the loudspeaker and buzz in each group one at a time. He'd never actually have to come in contact with them, unless he planned to give any of them a contract. His leads had been given him through his agents, who traveled all around leaving his cards with promising talents. This made the procedure much easier for him.

He decided to call in the James Gang first, since they had a few instruments to haul into the room, and he'd have to hold the buzzer down a little longer for them. The others were just vocal auditions for now. "Yo! James Gang!" he proclaimed over the speaker. "Get your stuff together and go on in. You're up!" The other groups all wished them luck as they brought in their stuff.

After listening to their brief audition, Derek crinkled his nose and sniffled. "What exactly was that? R&B, country and western, what gives?" The 2 bearded guys who'd played the guitars looked at each other for a moment. Derek was a little exasperated over the fact that aside from their obvious lack of talent good enough to earn them a record label, they weren't even organized enough to know what they were trying to play.

Finally the stockier of the 2 guitar players looked up. "I guess you could call it biker jazz," he said, with a sincerity which amused Derek at first, but then the more he thought about it, the more he realized it actually fit the description quite well.

"Hmm," he said, trying to compensate for telling them they were bad, while still hoping to figure out some way to help them click in the industry. After all, he truly believed no band that was good enough to audition for him had no potential, only the need for some revisions. Of course, in their case, a lot of those were needed.

"All right, guys. Hang out in the waiting room for a bit, okay? Let's see what these others have to offer, while I figure out if there's any way I can sign you guys." They happily brought their stuff back out, as Derek called in the Harmonettes.

This was definitely one sexy group of girls, and Derek knew this could bias him to some extent. But then the girls in the James Gang were also pretty hot, albeit tough looking and most likely taken by those 3 tougher looking guys as their significant others. Of course, Derek had always been able to be objective in his trade, regardless of the appearance of his talents. These were certainly not the first groups with attractive women, nor would they be the last.

Unfortunately, neither the Harmonettes nor the Torches sounded good enough for Derek to sign right now. But as he watched them all reconvene in the waiting room to eagerly await his answers for their burning desire to a record deal, an image suddenly froze in his mind. It was the most incredible visual experience he'd ever had. And based on his logic about seeking out potential in everyone that ever entered this building, he finally realized why sight was as important as sound. In fact, if there was ever a project that needed props, this was the one. Under most circumstances, the talents he cut deals with would appear on the album cover. But here was a case where the redone version of a great old musical commemorating its 40th anniversary on his label didn't quite live up to its visual standards. And in this game, an album's look always had to live up to its sound.

Of course, he had other people under him for this end of the profession, but since he was the boss, he'd now taken it upon himself to do it for the first time ever. He cleared his throat over the speaker as loud as he could before speaking up abruptly.

"Yo, groups! Freeze! All of you. Stay where you are. Don't move a muscle."

They all looked pretty startled but then seemed to realize Derek only had their best interests at heart. "Okay, everyone, relax. This isn't a robbery. I just want to see if I'm right."

"Right about what?" asked the toughest looking guitar player from the James Gang who'd spoken to him earlier.

"Look, do you all want a deal or don't you?"

"Yeah!" they yelled together.

'Sounds good,' thought Derek. "Then be quiet, stay still and let me study you for a bit!" Now they all relaxed, smiled and looked as natural as ever.

"So, let's see now, Brooklyn, yeah, 1957, yeah, planes versus fish, yeah! All right, I think we got our riff-raff! How would you all like to model?"

Although shocked at first, after hearing Derek's radical proposal, they each saw it as a great opportunity, to be pictured together on the album cover of the new West Side Story.

Has Anyone
Seen the Butler?

T he kitchen was spotless as usual. It was as if no meal had ever been prepared, no plans made. The banquet at the Windemere home had just sort of come and gone, like the falling star in the night which seemed to accompany it.

Of course, the GUESTS had been QUITE impressed, as always. The Windemeres DEFINITELY KNEW how to THROW a party, as well as party THEMSELVES. For a family who may have been on the outs, the SOLUTION could ALWAYS be found in one of their well-attended BASHES. It was as if they could REDEFINE RECONCILIATION.

Naturally, this made it practically IMPOSSIBLE for the upper crust in the community to GOSSIP. They would always have to say it had been a mere FABRICATION, NOTHING but A NASTY, SCANDALOUS RUMOR how the Windemeres had any SKELETONS currently living in their CLOSET. After all, how could they POSSIBLY host the FINEST functions in the COMMUNITY, appear together with nothing but the WARMEST receptiveness—both for their GUESTS, AND each OTHER, and BE in a QUICKLY DOWNSPRIRALING RELATIONSHIP? It just DIDN'T HOLD WATER.

The dancing had been lovely that evening, conversation was basically centered around the stock market, the price of caviar, and the types of provisions made in vacation villas the world over—that sort of stuff. Life seemed normal, happy and unified.

If any CRIME had been committed, all evidence of it certainly was scrubbed away with a fine-tooth comb. Yet even if there was no ACTUAL crime, only acts of COMPLETE NON-MORALITY, WHO would be the WISER?

The Windemere children were all asleep, perhaps dreaming of an upcoming ski trip in the Swiss Alps their parents had promised them. Or the SENSATIONAL RIDE on their father's corporate JET to GET them there. Or a multitude of OTHER possible PERKS which went with being heirs to one of the Fortune 500's most RENOWNED elite.

The servants were all in their own boudoirs located about the many extravagant suites on the estate, perhaps dreaming of any number of possible perks THEY had coming. Of course, simply being gainfully employed by the Windemeres was an extremely enviable advantage in and of itself—at least to the AVERAGE individual.

And of course, there was the estate itself— standing proud and true—representing itself as the STERLING PILLAR of the town. In its own regal splendor, an estate which not only spelled the entire COMMUNITY, but basically held it TOGETHER, for both economic and political purposes.

After all, it WAS the MOST prolific TOURIST attraction by FAR. Hundreds upon thousands of visitors would pass through the town ANNUALLY to catch themselves a GLIMPSE, though FEW entered.

After all, the Windemere estate was marked as a privileged site—a modern-day Holy Land. And only those considered the recipients of nobility were able to set foot on the property without the risk of being arrested or even SHOT at. Even the MAINTENANCE people who were summoned to WORK on the property from time to time needed a most special security clearance before entering the grounds.

And in actuality, these rules were enacted due to the strict ways of Mrs. Windemere, who had decided from day one to keep her priorities upheld to the letter. Some would even say she carried a quiet grudge against the mass of humanity, and in her style of introversion, could keep a better DISTANCE between herself and those whom she considered a threat to her way of life. Of course, these were only rumors based on her afore-mentioned habits. She still had lots of people in her life who loved her dearly, plenty of friends, and perhaps just the RIGHT amount of protectiveness over her best interests—the kind we might ALL be better off if we kept.

In any case, the party held in the Windemere home on that particular evening was still a fairly pleasant memory for her, as she brushed her long, flaxen hair before the vanity fair mirror in her chambers. Surely her man agreed, but the night was young.

He lay back in the king-size bed, his hands and mouth at the ready for the passion which was about to spell their evening. Just the SIGHT of her BACKSIDE wriggling in FRONT of him as she made herself as presentable as she COULD was enough to drive him WILD. Of course she was well aware of how their common DELAY tactics always made the lovemaking so much more rewarding in the end. In fact, the delay which had been the party earlier in the evening had caused them BOTH to fantasize QUITE VIVIDLY over what was NOW about to take place.

"Oh, Stanley, I'm SO READY for you! Perhaps like I've NEVER been BEFORE. The way your HIPS were bucking all EVENING down there, as every one of our guests could see nothing but our most CASUAL FACES! Isn't THIS ALWAYS what makes the LOVIN' so GOOD? All our PRIVATE LONGINGS and DESIRES. Don't we always work it in just so RIGHT?"

"Oh, YES! I've built every drop of PASSION up to a FEVER PITCH, my dear. And I won't STOP with YOU until EVERY LAST DROP is spent as COMPLETELY as it CAN be!" Their breathing was now as audible as their words.

"Oh, Stanley. You BETTER have made sure we're COMPLETELY UNDISTURBED. Because the way I'm feeling NOW, I wouldn't stop no matter WHAT!" He quickly double checked the wings' locked doors.

"Oh, YES, YEAH, YES, OH MORE, MORE, MORE!" Evelyn continued bucking with every bit of her rekindled strength, as Stanley performed like the champion of the long hump he was. As usual, their pleasure was the best kept secret from the estate, as nobody believed they were getting on so WELL.

Of course, there were some who suspected there might be a small amount of UNFAITHFULNESS between them, but naturally, these were merely nasty rumors among the locals—completely FABRICATED for the purpose of the GRATIFICATION which went with the sport of GOSSIP—and of course, it mattered VERY LITTLE to EITHER of them, ESPECIALLY at times like THIS.

But as the night moved on deliciously, they were so ENMESHED in their passion, they hardly heard the sound of what MIGHT have been a possible INTRUDER in their midst. They passed it off as MERELY the WIND whistling through the ALCOVE ABOVE them, and who or what else could it be? After all, everyone was where they were SUPPOSED to be now, nobody within any REACH of disturbing them. Yet after awhile they realized there WAS in fact, someone winding through the hallway with INCREASING SPEED, which prompted Stanley to draw his gun and FIRE FATALLY on a suspecting Mr. Windemere as he walked in on them after changing all the locks in the wing, making TWICE TRUE the most POPULAR phrase, the BUTLER did it.

Valley Miracle

Through thick and thin. For better or worse. In sickness and in health. 'Til DEATH do them off. These are some of the most important anecdotes which keep the state of life intact. And there in the valley, all of them were stretched to the limit.

The drought had brought multitudes of misfortune for many months. All the prosperity which was ever-present since the area had been settled as the fertilest land in the county back some 3 generations ago, seemed like it could only be returned by the waking up from the nightmare. The residents were in shock. If only this acrid dust bowl would receive some rain. Even another brushfire starting thunderstorm would be most welcome, if there could be but some MOISTURE to go along with it.

Sue and Willie had literally watched their wine grapes go from ripe and ready, to blue and dead in a period of less than 3 weeks. It was the stuff that spelled depression, and even the special cultivation tactics they'd tried had proven completely fruitless. There were unshared thoughts of suicide between them. The vineyard was their livelihood; it had always been. Without it they were nothing. They represented their bottles of the finest Chablis in the land, the way Goliath represented the credo of the proud giant. And without the means to keep making them, it might as well have been the slingshot fired flush between their eyes.

Through it all, it seemed the only one with any shred of optimism in the whole valley was grandpa. He'd seen this valley through thick and thin since its founding all those years ago. He always considered it the most sacred land on earth—truly God's country—never possibly prone to any kinds of misfortune and/or upheaval.

Of course, everyone knew grandpa had reached the point in his life where his mind had become a vast jungle, containing all but what was considered reality. And in spite of this, everyone in the valley still loved and respected him the way they always had. Especially his family. Which is why they had a most difficult time trying to figure out what to do about him.

"What are we going to do about him?" Sue asked Willie one parching day, as he kneeled before the couple of hundred feet of shriveled vines, which aside from the few hundred or so dead grapes lying around on the property, were about the only sign of what had once been fertile plant life. "It's getting to the point where I'm ready to go out there and JOIN him in his RITUAL! I mean, it's not like there's much other recourse, if you THINK about it."

Willie stood before the window, wiping the clinging sweat from his brow into the hot, arid air. "Don't think I haven't."

They continued to watch him as he moaned like a swami, soft at first but then louder and louder, until he accompanied the moans by jumping up and down in the vineyard, then rolling around on the ground, then jumping, then rolling and moaning..

"You know, Sue, I wonder if we could get people from outside the valley to come and pay us good money to watch this stuff."

"WILLIE! How can you even THINK such a thing? Or is this just your most SICK WAY of trying to keep up our morale with an INSANE brand of WARPED HUMOR?"

"Well, Sue, you know the bottom line is that we ARE just about practically BROKE. And while the VINEYARD IS our WHOLE LIFE...."

"You JERK! The VINEYARD IS OUR WHOLE LIFE!" Willie tried to regroup his thoughts before resuming what he was about to say.

"LIKE I WAS SAYING, Sue. I KNOW the VINE-YARD is our WHOLE LIFE, BUT!" He looked at her carefully before continuing to make sure she wasn't going to interrupt him before he made his point. "We DO NEED MONEY, OKAY? MONEY, DINERO, MOOLAH, GREENSTUFF."

"OKAY, ALL RIGHT, I KNOW." He knew she was just frustrated.

"I don't know, Sue. Maybe this IS a matter above our hands. Maybe the gods want us to do something miraculous for THEM, in return for THEM doing something miraculous for US and our grapes. And maybe the only ALTERNATIVE IS to appease them. Perhaps we should make love, what do you think?"

Sue had never looked more flabbergasted. Perhaps Willie had taken these events way too seriously. After all, dust bowls would always come and go, but common decency needed to be maintained throughout. "I really don't think that's a good idea, Willie."

"Why not? I thought you were with me all the way with this."

"Not that much. Considering that we ARE brother and sister!"

"Yeah, you're probably right. I suppose the only thing the gods would do is LAUGH at us. I mean after all, if they were mean enough to cause this drought, I guess shocking them into ENDING it probably ISN'T the answer."

"Oh, Willie. I'm SO glad YOU haven't taken total leave of your senses, after all. I mean at least GRANDPA'S got his AGE, and all his years on this property finally adding up as a valid EXCUSE for losing his mind, but YOU, YOU'RE still quite young and smart, and there's probably more time than we THINK to figure out a REAL SOUND ALTERNATIVE to this crisis."

Before he could answer, Willie noticed that grandpa was now yelping louder than ever. "Oh, my GOD! Maybe we SHOULD go out there and bring him inside. Before any of the NEIGHBORS finally tries to have him carted off." Sue couldn't have agreed more.

But as they both ran outside to grab grandpa, they noticed a most AMAZING occurrence. COULD IT BE? The ground on which grandpa bucked about had suddenly become quite saturated. In fact, WATER was now filling up the land so FAST, that GRANDPA was no longer just ROLLING or BUCKING, he was SWIMMING! And as Willie and Sue found themselves knee-deep, and then WAIST-DEEP in the swirling stream, they suddenly feared they might all be DROWNED, if they couldn't get a hold of grandpa, and THEN somehow find a way to float themselves to the PITCH in the VALLEY, where the water would NO LONGER be CARRYING them DOWNHILL!

"Grandpa, COME ON! TAKE MY HAND!" yelled Willie, reaching out to him. Sue reached her OWN hand out to Willie.

"Hey, what about ME, Willie? Can't I take your hand? I don't swim so good EITHER, you know."

"Sure, sis, the more the merrier." And then they were off to their final plateau of safety, from which they were able to wade onto solid ground and contemplate why and what had just happened.

Of course, they never did make head or tails of it. All the valley residents were SO GRATE-FUL; however THEIR VINEYARD was completely RUINED. So with the drought over, their lives in a shambles even though the valley was once again fertile, the 3 of them found peace and reverence as monks in a Tibetan monastery.

Lick 'Em, Stick 'Em

B een to the post office lately? That's an inter-
esting one. Seems like a pretty weird survey
question, DON'T it? But what the hey day. If it
wasn't WEIRD, it wouldn't grab YOUR ATTENTION,
now WOULD it?

And of COURSE, THAT'S been MY intention
all ALONG. WHY? Well, MAYBE it's because I
want to know what all YOU people think of some
of the newest STAMPS out there. WHY? Well maybe it's because I DESIGNED a few of them. OR,
maybe it's because I'm promoting PHILATELY.
Of course, YOU'LL never know what I'm GETTING
at, if you don't KEEP READING, now, WILL you?

Now PERHAPS that seems rather MANIPULA-
TIVE, HUH? But WHAT an AWESOME SITUATION,
RIGHT? I mean, HERE I AM, asking YOU about the
LAST time you've been to the POST OFFICE. And
I'm SO VAGUE and WISHY-WASHY about WHY.
And YET, YOU'RE probably so CURIOUS that you
KEEP READING this shit. Isn't that WONDERFUL?
I mean, you KNOW what could HAPPEN here. This
is a SHORT STORY, after all. There's ONLY a FEW
PAGES to GO. And at THIS POINT in the story, there
are 2 POSSIBLE CASE SCENARIOS—the WORST
and the BEST! The WORST being that YOU could
READ this ENTIRE STORY and HATE it. Of course,
that would only be YOUR worse case scenario.
MINE would be of course, if you happened to pick

up the BOOK that THIS story is CONTAINED in, start reading THIS story, and think FUCK THIS!

Of course, you probably ARE thinking that. So let me REPHRASE that. The worse case scenario for ME would be if you're no longer READING this, at THIS POINT.

But if you're NOT, then LOOK WHAT THE FUCK YOU'D BE MISSING! My HARD HITTING and SUPERFLUOUS EXPLANATIONS about the SCIENCE of MANIPULATION. And HOW I can CHOOSE to jump BACK and FORTH and FORTH and BACK from the MAIN topic of this story at WILL, and YOU'RE all still INTO it a THOUSAND fuckin' PERCENT! Now AIN'T THAT A KICK?

But I think you REALIZE I haven't ABAN-DONED the MAIN topic of this STORY at ALL. Which is WHY you're still HERE. You're just WAITING for me to CONNECT it with the CRAP I began the story WITH. You know, the stuff about the damn POST OFFICE! Well, in the words of the WILD WICKED WITCH of the WEST, ALL IN GOOD TIME, my pretty, ALL IN GOOD TIME. Of course, I know you can't ALL be pretty, in fact, I know a LOT of you are fuckin' UGLY TOO. But THAT'S the BEAUTY of it. HMM. How IRONIC, finding BEAUTY in UGLY. NO, NO, NO! Not YOUR beauty. ITS beauty. It being the SITUATION! AND the SITUATION being the FACT that I KNOW all ABOUT you. At least THOSE of you I have in my POWER! YES, you READ THAT QUITE RIGHT — IN!

MY! POWER! AH HAH! NOW, you're thinking. NOW he'll EXPLAIN to us what that's got to DO with the fuckin' POST OFFICE!

YO! Molly! Molly McBride! Yeah, that's right, I'm talkin' to YOU there, Molly McBride. Molly McBride, age 26 of Pittsfield, Massachusetts. HO! HO! YO HO, HO, TIME OUT NOW a SECOND, TIME! FUCKIN! OUT! WHOOSH! I almost FORGOT! This is JUST FICTION! And of COURSE that MEANS I'd better PROTECT myself from any kind of fuckin' LAWSUIT before I go any FURTHER. HOW YOU SAY? By reminding ALL of you, but especially YOU there, Molly McBride, age 26 of Pittsfield, Massachusetts, assuming there really IS SUCH a type, or TYPES if it turns out there ARE in FACT, more than ONE of you, how ANY RESEMBLANCE TO ANYONE IN THIS FUCKIN' STORY TO ANY OTHER ONE LIVING OR fuckin' DEAD, IS PURELY COINCIDANCE. Ain't that cute how I SPELLED it like "DANCE" on the end? Makes it seem almost kind of ELEGANT don't it? You know like ELE GANT. Well ANYWAY, I THINK you know what I'm GETTING at HERE. I'm referring to ONE SPECIAL CHARACTER in my STORY here, but in CASE it turns out there really IS a Molly McBride of Pittsfield, Massachusetts, age 26, or even MORE than ONE Molly McBride of Pittsfield, Massachusetts, age 26, the LAST thing I need is a fuckin' SLANDER suit HOISTED upon ME. SO THERE. And now that THAT little formality is out of the way, MAY? I?

PROCEED? THANK you.

Okay, so Molly, how was it you happened to be giving HEAD to that guy you met at Trudi's last night, that DISGUSTING PERVERT?

Oh, by the WAY, Trudi's is a fictitious BAR in the town of Pittsfield, Massachusetts. Or CLUB if you will. Or even if you WON'T. But the point is, if Trudi's IS a real place in the town of Pittsfield, Massachusetts, it's as COINCIDENTAL as Molly McBride, age 26 of Pittsfield, Massachusetts. Just covering my BUTT CRACK, YOU understand. Of course, the town of Pittsfield, Massachusetts, is real enough. I should know; I don't live so far away from it. And the actual population is let's see now.... OH, WHAT THE FUCK AM I DOING? I GOT A STORY TO BELT OUT, HERE! Just stalling for TIME I SUPPOSE. ANYWAY!

The Molly McBride in THIS story was at Trudi's the other night at about 10 or so in the evening, trying to make a singles connection, I GUESS. BY DAY she works as a BANK teller in, yup that's right you GUESSED it, Pittsfield, Massachusetts (NOW I no LONGER have to add these COINCIDENCE footnotes, THANK fuckin' GOD) and she also happened to have to stop at the POST OFFICE (AH, HAH!) YESTERDAY to PICK up some STAMPS and mail a letter.

Now as it TURNS out, she happened to SEE that guy at Trudi's for the FIRST time during her visit there the other NIGHT. He'd been rather OBSCENE

with her, I found out, not so much in his CON-
VERSATION with her about the WEATHER and such,
BUT in the way he RUBBED HIS DICK as he
DISCUSSED it. Didn't impress Molly much.

By NOW I'll bet your wondering how I KNOW
this stuff. And I'm MORE than happy to let you
KNOW how, as it will SURELY connect all that
STUFF about the POST OFFICE. Okay. HERE GOES.
I HAVE in FACT, been able to MANUFACTURE and
DISTRIBUTE a VERY SPECIAL TYPE of POSTAGE
STAMP. So far, it's still in the EXPERIMENTAL
stage. I've sent it around to a few post offices. But
NOW after seeing how fuckin' EFFECTIVE it is,
you'd better BELIEVE I'll be WIDENING the
distribution CONSIDERABLY. And WHAT'S so
SPECIAL about this PARTICULAR STAMP? Simple.
It's HYPNOTIC. Puts ANYONE who LICKS it COM-
PLETELY in my fuckin' POWER. AND it ALSO
enables me to READ THEIR MINDS. Thus, when
Molly McBride licked one of my stamps at the post
office YESTERDAY, and was totally REPULSED by
the guy at Trudi's from the night BEFORE, I
SUGGESTED to her that if the guy should show up
again the next time, she should do WHATEVER he
WANTS with him. So NOW I'm having GREAT FUN
with my project.

I guess you could call me a MATCHMAKER of
sorts. Because, I also have a Reginald Salamander
of Akron, Ohio, under my power.

Great NAME HUH? Remember JUST FICTION,

ONLY COINCIDENCE. Anyway, he's divorced with 2 kids. And I think I'll bring he and Molly together soon. See where THAT leads. Of course, not until after he fucks some horny old hag 3 times his age. Hey, I've got to have SOME fun. After all, manipulation IS the spice of LIFE.

Tree Me

O nce upon a time, I was a woodcarver. Now THAT sounds like the start of a fairytale, doesn't it? But if there were any fairies around back then (and I MEAN that STRICTLY in the COLLOQUIAL sense — LIVE and LET live, I really DO BELIEVE that) but of COURSE, like I was starting to INDICATE, it was FROWNED upon MUCH MORE during those years, as was just about ANY form of eccentric lifestyle. In FACT, even I was considered rather OFF in my time. Not in the sense that I had any unusual PREFERENCES, as THOSE were all pretty much CONFORMIST. But in the sense that I had lots of UNUSUAL IDEAS which at that TIME didn't really WASH or bode WELL with the MAJORITY of the POPULATION.

The earth was ROUND, the sky was ENDLESS, I could hum better than any HUMMINGBIRD in the land, THOSE sorts of ideas. Of course I'M STILL pretty convinced those FIRST 2 are TRUE, although I don't know how good I can HUM anymore since I haven't actually DONE so in a few hundred years. But I'm TRYING. And SOMEDAY maybe I'll pull that FLAME from the FIRE and shock the WORLD. Of course pulling FLAMES from FIRE with my BARE HANDS was something ELSE I could DO quite well at one time. Yet THIS was merely an ILLUSION which I'd MANAGED to perfect through YEARS of PRACTICE. However, what made the difference between my CONTEMPORARIES BURNING me at the STAKE for practicing WITCHCRAFT and NOT was my GREAT TALENT.

You see I existed during the Renaissance, a time when people had just begun to believe in the power of ART. And BELIEVE me, it's a STRONG POWER. It's relieved MANY of MUCH PERSECUTION over time. As well as giving THOSE of us who were BLESSED with its POTENTIAL, the ABILITY to MAINTAIN RESPECT while REMAINING EXPRES-SIVE, 2 VERY IMPORTANT TRAITS which NEVER seemed to STABILIZE during the Middle Ages.

MY friend, Leonardo would agree SOUNDLY, were there some way for HIM to be RESURRECTED. Of course, I never cared much for the sight of Mona, yet I'd have fought TOOTH and NAIL for the RIGHTS of her SUPPORTERS! Of course, as I'd PREVIOUSLY INDICATED, the power of ART was such a STRONG NOBILITY, that those of us who'd been BLESSED with it, stood FIRE and BRIMSTONE above the rest, as being held in AWE as we were, allowed us to keep our RESPECT and DIGNITY, without having to spill any BLOOD—whether it be our OWN, or that of our OPPRESSORS.

Of course THIS gave THOSE of us who DID care to dabble in the black arts from time to time, a SPECIAL EDGE, as I believe would be the CORRECT VERNACULAR TODAY in describing our PRAC-TICE. The reason this was SO was that EVERY-THING we DID would ALWAYS be CONSIDERED for the BENEFIT of MANKIND, and after a THOUSAND YEARS of PLAGUE and RAT-INFESTED, HIDEOUS, SHORTENED LIFE, it was TRUE.

I know for a FACT, the practice of MAGIC during THIS era was ALWAYS for the benefit of MANKIND. And WOMANKIND TOO. In FACT, through ALL MY YEARS deploying the practice of MAGIC, I MANAGED to CREATE a MAGICAL MASTERPIECE, which has to THIS DAY, become LEGENDARY. As I ALSO have created ANOTHER such MASTERPIECE, which while it's NOT become LEGENDARY, has ENABLED me to CONTINUE to EXIST, and have ALL the KNOWLEDGE of WORLD-LY EVENTS including my OWN FOLKLORE, which PROVIDES me with the MEANS to form my OWN OPINIONS and JUDGMENTS. Yet NOT MUCH ELSE! At least not YET.

However, getting back to my ORIGINAL masterpiece of MAGIC, which has made me

LEGENDARY, I've actually spent MOST of the past half-MILLENNIUM, trying to figure out why it was MISCONSTRUED so. In OTHER words, in the LEGEND I've been PORTRAYED as a lonely WOOD-CUTTER, and THAT much was TRUE. But I BELIEVE because of MANY ROMAN CATHOLIC VALUES, which COMPLETELY FROWNED upon ANY ACTS of LURID RELEASE which did NOT occur between SPOUSES for the BENEFIT of PROCREATION, MY legend was altered DRASTICALLY. As I'd ALREADY INDICATED, my ARTISTIC TALENT kept me from LOSING my LIFE to the FLAMES of ANGRY VILLAGERS, HOWEVER, for the ACTS I HAD COMMITTED myself to, I had my OWN LEGEND of HUMAN TRANSFORMATION COMPLETELY ALTERED, for the purpose of MORALS of the CHURCH staying INTACT. I SUPPOSE I should be GRATEFUL that this was ALL that resulted.

Yet NOW I feel it's time I set the record STRAIGHT, as those of you at the turn of the 20th century would say. As I DO so, I ask you all to bear WITH me, for based on my knowledge of popular folklore in this day and age, and the AFTER effects of RADICAL MEDIA COVERAGE—which of COURSE is a LUXURY that those living in MY time never had—although to this DAY, I see MUCH FEAR, SHOCK and HEARTACHE coming to pass as a RESULT of it—and I TRULY FEEL that upon hearing MY version of my OWN, MOST FONDLY REMEMBERED STORY, which of course is the

TRUTHFUL account of what took PLACE with myself and my CREATION, I KNOW there'll be MUCH SHOCK, and perhaps DISMAY as WELL. Yet I KNOW how much of an EMPHASIS is put on TRUTH these days, even though the AFORE-MENTIONED EFFECTS of LEARNING it is SO COMMON! However, as I'D always been one who enjoyed SHOCKING OTHERS at every OPPOR-TUNITY, I TRULY FEEL that it will ACTUALLY mean QUITE an ENJOYABLE PURGE. I mean, it's NOT like the WORLD will come to an END when you REALIZE what I've been ABOUT for all these CENTURIES. In FACT, based on the most POPULAR TYPE of today's MIND set, I NOW venture to think my TRUE account of my LEGEND will be found rather ENJOYABLE. I SIMPLY HAD to PREPARE you for the AFTERSHOCK before I BEGAN. After ALL, I may have been a RADICAL in my day, but NEVER was I a SCOUNDREL. To THIS DAY, I'm STILL the type who believes in a STRONG BUILDUP.

So NOW you have it. Therefore, I BELIEVE you're FINALLY READY for the TRUTH. All I ASK is that you pay CAREFUL ATTENTION to the ALTERED details of my STORY, as I RELATE to them, and SEE if my THEORIES for the REASONS for those alterations don't hold WATER.

It began innocently enough one day, when I decided to try to construct a DOLL, which was AESTHETICALLY PLEASING as WELL as a sight to BEHOLD! In OTHER words, IT would be in the guise of a SHE, and SHE would BE the most EXQUISITE DOLL in the VILLAGE. SHE would be more APPEALING—at LEAST from a VISUAL position than ANY LIVING WOMAN in the VILLAGE! Which she absolutely WAS. In FACT, while she had MANY ADMIRERS who'd come to OBSERVE and make COMMENTARY, she ALSO had MANY ENVIOUS observers—PRIMARILY those WOMEN in the village who'd be UNABLE to hold a CANDLE to her. I named her Panache, meaning FLAMBOYANT, STYLISH, THAT sort of thing. Suffice it to say, when she MIRACULOUSLY came to LIFE one day, to FULFILL my LONELINESS, it spawned an AMAZINGLY GROTESQUE account of a PUPPET turning into a BOY, whose NOSE kept GROWING. Which I'm SURE was SIMPLY the most DISGUSTING fabrication of my PHALLIC FULFILLMENT by the village MULTITUDE OF JEALOUS MAIDENS.

THERE you have it. My FIRST magical masterpiece. My second, very quickly, was a new type of WOOD I found to make my CASKET, which somehow PRESERVED me and grew into a most SPECIAL TREE!

A Most Heartfelt Situation

Reinhold had been waiting for this day, virtually his whole life. He'd been BORN into a family of the BIGGEST BASEBALL fans. In fact WHILE he was born, his MOTHER was DELIBERATELY CROUCHED in a CATCHER'S position, hoping it would INFLUENCE him to PLAY baseball someday. And his FATHER had been there, the second that Reinhold had opened his EYES, asking the doctor if he could TELL if his VISION was as good as Ted Williams' eyesight had been. Of course, there was no way he could know at THAT point, yet he could CERTAINLY APPRECIATE Reinhold's parents' ATTITUDE, being the doctor HIMSELF was a season TICKET holder.

Naturally, his parents tried to make SURE Reinhold could BAT and THROW before he could walk or talk. And for all intents and purposes it paid OFF quite WELL. By his THIRD BIRTHDAY, Reinhold had played EVERY POSITION with his family out in their back yard, had made accurate, albeit relatively short THROWS from all of them on COMMAND, AND had ACTUALLY hit the ball over the FENCE MANY times. Of course, that was ONLY for a distance of about 12 FEET; HOWEVER it was QUITE OBVIOUS the kid had NATURAL TALENT, and even MORE obvious what his INTENTIONS were for when he grew up. Which NATURALLY gave every member of his FAMILY and all his little

FRIENDS, the opportunity to be ABLE to someday live out their OWN dreams vicariously through Reinhold.

Even his NAME gave the indication of the most WELL-ROUNDED athlete—Reinhold Baxter Barrett—the moniker had Hall Of Fame, BEER, SNEAKER, CAR, TRUCK, and whatever OTHER type of possible ENDORSEMENTS his future AGENT would find him the BENEFITS for, written ALL OVER it. As he grew up, the other kids came up with SO MANY DIFFERENT NICKNAMES for him—REINIE, HOLDER, REINBAR, BAXIE, BAXETT, HOLDBAX, etc. that by the TIME he'd reached his FIRST YEAR in SEMI-PRO, he had more choices for THOSE than he had for his BATTING stance. So this basically had become the CREDO this young star, who played every position, batted way over .300, struck out way fewer than 50 times, yet hit way over 30 home runs, batted in way over 100 RBIs, slugged way over .400 and fielded way over .900, had to LIVE with. The decision of which NAME to use. Which of course, gave members of the media following him the chance to use their OWN CHOICES of names, after each game of HEROIC proportion in which he PLAYED during their COMMENTARY. Finally, one day a most RENOWNED SPORTS reporter stated how he'd YET to see a kid out there play with as much HEART, as Reinhold Baxter Barrett. And being that some of the reporter's COLLEAGUES THEN pointed out that THIS was ACTUALLY the FIRST time they'd SEEN the kid's ENTIRE NAME used in an article, and it REMINDED them of when Howard Cosell spoke of JACKIE ROOSEVELT ROBINSON, AND, it made them feel TINGLY all OVER because it was a moment which CLEARLY defined DESTINY, AND it was a WORD (HEART that IS) which had EVERY LETTER from his GIVEN NAME in it, MEANING that it could BE the new NICKNAME for the KID! AND, when this PARTICULAR reporter took his colleagues' SUGGESTION to HEART, (NO INTENDED PUN) because following THAT PAR-TICULAR BALLGAME, which had put Reinhold Baxter Barrett's TEAM in the position where the NEXT WIN would mean them WINNING the CHAMPIONSHIP, where SCOUTS of EVERY MAJOR LEAGUE TEAM would be watching HIM, to see what kind of BONUS offer they'd be willing to MAKE him, that reporter took it upon himself to refer to Reinhold Baxter Barrett as HEART in the post-game INTERVIEW, to SEE how the nickname TOOK with the kid.

And when the reporter nonchalantly AP-PROACHED Reinhold Baxter Barrett after the game, and said, "Great game, HEART. What did you DO out there today which ENABLED you to hit those 2 TRIPPERS, including the GAME winner, and also to peg out that guy Strashius with that OFF-BALANCE throw from centerfield, which would have at LEAST TIED the game, and PROBABLY brought in the winning run for THEM?

And how did it FEEL, HEART? And one more question, HEART. What do you think of the team's CHANCES of winning it ALL tomorrow? And what MAJOR LEAGUE CLUB do YOU want to PLAY for? Oh, SORRY, HEART, I guess that was 2 more questions. But what of it?"

And since at that moment, Reinhold Baxter Barrett not only did NOT turn around and SLUG that reporter in the MOUTH, or even anywhere ELSE, or even QUESTION him about WHY he'd been calling him HEART, but INSTEAD, answered the reporter's EVERY QUESTION with the ENTHUSIASM of the most HUMBLE kind of SUPERSTAR, then it became ESTABLISHED on THAT AFTERNOON, OFFICIALLY even, that from then ON, HEART would be the established NICKNAME of one Reinhold Baxter Barrett. And what that MEANT was, that beginning with the NEXT DAY'S BALLGAME, in which Reinhold Baxter Barrett would play CENTERFIELD, and of course do his BEST to not ONLY give his TEAM the CHAMPIONSHIP, BUT LAND possibly the BIGGEST ROOKIE BONUS for himself in the HISTORY of MAJOR LEAGUE BASEBALL, all the OFFICIAL SCORING would be done at LEAST as far as Reinhold Baxter Barrett was concerned, using the name HEART. The LINEUP card would READ HEART, batting cleanup and playing center. The MANAGER and the other members of the team would yell for HEART to GO, and WAY to go, HEART, whenever a PLAY in the game involved

HIM. Members of the MEDIA covering the game would write HEART in their columns and SPEAK of HEART to each OTHER as they CONFERRED on the game. Of COURSE, the SCOUTS at the game would be BRIEFED during the PREGAME about HEART, the local RADIO broadcaster doing the game would refer to him as HEART, as would his FAMILY and FRIENDS, as they cheered him ON, from the STANDS, the PRESS BOX or WHATEVER GREAT LOCATION they happened to FINAGLE themselves for the game.

Suffice it to say, the EXCITEMENT in the life of Reinhold Baxter Barrett, had never been HIGHER than during the next 15 HOURS or so, and this was ALSO the case for the OTHER people mentioned in the PREVIOUS PARAGRAPH of this STORY, who of COURSE, do not bear REPEATING.

And as the game BEGAN, the excitement CONTINUED to BUILD and BUILD, as it WAS EXACTLY the type of GAME which EVERYONE who'd felt they had a STAKE in it ANTICIPATED. The ZEROS kept piling up INNING after INNING, as BOTH STARTING PITCHERS had had MARVELOUS STUFF. Reinhold Baxter Barrett managed the game's first HIT with one out in the 5TH with a tough infield SINGLE on which a SLOWER guy probably would have been thrown OUT, yet never made it to SECOND as a BANG BANG double play snuffed out the inning. But then in the top of the 9TH, the game still SCORELESS, he GUNNED out the go ahead RUN at the plate on a GREAT inning ending PLAY.

After leading off the BOTTOM of the 9th with a SINGLE, and going to SECOND on a FIELDER'S CHOICE, Reinhold Baxter Barrett scored the WINNING RUN on a GREAT SLIDE into HOME on another SINGLE. Yet the JOY ENDED as the CATCHER DIED of cardiac arrest, making it a first as a HEART stopped a heart on the DIAMOND.

Moon Bright

I t's a JUNGLE out there. In the STREETS, the ALLEYS, behind the PARKED CARS, where people go to RECREATE in the night. All the people with their FAMILIES and FRIENDS, trying to live their lives with the FREEDOM and LIBERTY upon which THIS GREAT LAND was FOUNDED!

Yet somehow, the LINE is so THIN between the OPPORTUNITIES for making GOOD, HONEST USE of the situation and RADICALLY VIOLATING the rights of OTHERS who are EASY PREY for the NASTINESS which often LURKS out there, waiting for JUST the right MOMENT to POUNCE and VICTIMIZE. And I KNOW that if you're out there in MY neighborhood with EVIL on your MINDS on the wrong NIGHT, YOU YOURSELF may end up a VICTIM. YES, THAT'S RIGHT. YOU there. Young

MUGGERS and GANGBANGERS who THINK that EVERYTHING they want is SIMPLY for the TAKING. Well it ISN'T. And it's taken ME MANY years to figure out WHY it isn't. In OTHER words, the MAIN thing is that over the PAST many years, I've been TRYING to form an IMAGE in my mind. An IMAGE of THUGS passing through, ready to PROCURE their EVIL on the INNOCENT. And it's been QUITE a LONG, HARD STRUGGLE for me. So WHAT have I DONE about it? Not a THING. Because NOW I realize that no matter what HAPPENS I'll NEVER be ABLE to see ANY of those HOODLUMS. But I ALSO realize it doesn't MATTER. I'll STILL be FINE! HOW? Well, HERE'S my STORY.

It began many MOONS ago, when I lived in a charming village in the OLD country. I was but a simple laborer, with no dreams of WEALTH, LOVE or PERSONAL SUPERIORITY, only to be able to keep the RESPECT and DIGNITY of my fellow villagers.

Then one day, SHE came along. She WAS truly BEAUTIFUL, and at FIRST I was QUITE TAKEN with the temptation of her MANY CHARMS. But it didn't take me long to see how SHALLOW and SUPER-FICIAL she really WAS—her position of ROYALTY not withstanding.

You see, in the Countess Marishnaquy I'd begun to see myself as MORE than a mere LABORER for the first time. I NOW saw myself as one who COULD actually have been of NOBLE STATURE—as one who COULD perhaps have woken up one

morning and found I'd been TRANSFORMED into a
GRAND PRINCE! The Countess had such a WAY
about her, in those WORDS of WOO and PASSION
she'd often SPEAK to me. Of course, NATURALLY
it reached the point when I'd found myself
THOROUGHLY ENTRANCED, and of course, what
ORDINARY MORTAL MAN WOULDN'T? The
Countess was as ELOQUENT as she was BEAUTIFUL,
and to be ACCOSTED by her from her PASSING
CARRIAGE, as I labored TIRELESSLY about the
streets of Budapest quickly caused the types of
SENSATIONS most MORTAL men only DREAMED
of. Suffice it to SAY, I was QUITE taken, and upon
being ORDERED by the Countess into her carriage,
how could I resist the CHANCE?

What followed at that time was the LOVELIEST
afternoon — a day of SHEER DELIGHT. We'd begun
with the most LUXURIOUS CARAVAN to the
ESTATE of the Countess, while along the way
sipping the most VINTAGE wines and sampling
SUPERB caviar. The VIEW of the world from my
new vantage point was one of PURE HEAVEN, as
though I had perhaps DIED and become an ANGEL
with NOW the chance to OBSERVE the world I left
behind with an AMAZINGLY ELEGANT rapture. Of
course, when the Countess and I arrived, I was
EQUALLY as taken with my NEW surroundings.
Though I'd never EXPERIENCED any desire to
observe ROYALTY in its NATURAL HABITAT, I'd
NOW reached a very special plateau from which

I never would have BELIEVED such GRAND sensations were possible. At LEAST for MYSELF. Of course, THIS was only the BEGINNING. The EXTREME PASSION of which the Countess would prove herself CAPABLE to me, sparked a FRENZY of desire I NEVER even knew I POSSESSED. I SIMPLY HAD to keep HAVING her OVER and OVER. As for ON THAT DAY, I learned FIRST HAND of the SHEER JOY of being a MAN!

However, as time went on, and my most PRIZED principles of SIMPLICITY began to RETURN to me, I found I could no LONGER keep up with the Countess. Parties in her palace each EVENING with all the ROYAL members of her DOMAIN as well as spending EVERY WAKING AND SEDATED MOMENT with her was SOON giving me SHEER HEARTACHE!

I KNEW there was simply NO MANNER in which I could let her down EASILY. I realized it was either a matter of bearing TRUTH and HEARTACHE, OR finding the most PERFECT moment to escape her HOLD as a RAT would try to escape the MOAT. Being the GENTLEMAN I was, and STILL AM TO-DAY I LIKE to believe, I chose to go forth to her in her private chambers and EXPLAIN to the Countess, the dilemma of my position.

However, before I was able to SEIZE the opportunity, I found her to be SUDDENLY ORDER-ING ME AROUND like a SLAVE or a SPOUSE to one who was CONSIDERABLY SOMEWHAT LESS than

ROYALTY. "You shall go DIRECTLY into the VILLAGE and PREPARE ME for this EVENING'S affair. I MUST LOOK as STUNNING as I am ABLE, and our GUESTS must be as WELL FED as that as WELL. So, THEREFORE, you are to ACQUIRE all the NECESSITIES for the OCCASION, MY FORMAL WEAR, OUR DINNER, and YOUR formal wear alike. Have you not BEEN YOURSELF to the HABER-DASHER'S establishment of late? You must REMEMBER EXACTLY whom you're REPRESENT-ING once you've been PERSONALLY SELECTED by the Countess, HERSELF, you know. You MUST NEVER FORGET what an ENVIABLE POSITION YOU ARE IN, SIR!"

She had NOW made me DOWNRIGHT FURIOUS! The NERVE of her, to try to PERMEATE the notion that I was QUITE SO FORTUNATE that she should REFER to herself as some SUPREME BEING on the MOMENT.

Aside from THIS blatant outrage, the Countess ALSO expected of me ALL the FUNDING for said goods and services, knowing FULL WELL I was STILL a SIMPLE LABORER, regardless of her most CHOICE recent SELECTION of me as her PERSONAL CARETAKER! "Madam, you OPENLY REPULSE ME!" I stated to her quite evenly, in no manner CONCERNED with any POSSIBLE CONSEQUENCE. As her DEMANDING DEMEANOR quickly turned to one of SHOCK and HORROR, I PROMPTLY let my-self out of her PALACE, away from her ESTATE, and after HAILING a carriage, was returned again to the life of LABORIOUS FREEDOM I had LONGED to once MORE regale.

Of course, I suppose I SHOULD have been WARY of when I was LEAVING her establishment, the Countess POINTING at me, yelling, "CURSE YOU! YOU WILL BE CURSED! FOREVER! MARK MY WORDS. YOU WILL BE CURSED!" While I HAD simply laughed it off, it SOON occurred to me when the MOON was full and I'd BLACK OUT until MORNING, THEN find out how one or MORE persons in the VILLAGE was MAULED to DEATH by some HIDEOUS HAIRY CREATURE, perhaps I SHOULD have taken some HEED in her warning. The TRUE SIGN was when I lived WELL into the 20th century, came to America, and read of some in MY neighborhood meeting the same fate, MANY HOODLUMS. Though I've killed some INNOCENT people, I SEEM to deter CRIME, and as I've led a LONG, CHARMED LIFE, a silver bullet does NOT scare me.

A Far-reaching
Coastal Dilemma

R ay and Fay Way were a very special couple. They'd met at the famous huge arch structure in the city of St. Louis, Missouri, which more or less indicates the midpoint of the United States of America. Immediately they'd begun to explore the possibilities of dating each other when the discussion began about how their first names sounded so much alike, how their first and last names would sound so much more alike if they were married, and Fay were to take Ray's last name, and the fact that each of them had wanted to see this particular structure for most of their lives, as it was most definitely the first and only kind of structure with such a monumental representation which they each knew about. So right away, they'd found some important things they had in common.

Ray was a hiker from the East Coast, New York City, to be exact. He had survived with nothing but his backpack, the bare necessity contents therein, a few hundred dollars in traveler's checks he was able to earn while surviving as an ice cream vendor in New York for the past couple of summers, and his feet and his thumb when his feet became tired. Fay was a biker from Southern California, around Los Angeles to be approximate. Her goal was to train for the Tour de France, and what better way than to get in these kinds of miles. They obviously seemed a pretty good match.

Aside from those other things, they also prided themselves in having a keen sense of direction. So much so, that when they'd EACH set out to go cross-country, they'd decided NOT to EVER ask

ANYONE which was the way to so and so. They'd simply follow their natural instincts, figuring out the time zones they were in by the sun's position, and when they discovered they'd reached the OCEANS bordering their destinations, they'd know they had arrived. And this had worked out PERFECTLY for them the first time, as they hadn't met until they were each on their way back home.

And it didn't take them long to discover a fun new diversion with each other—name games. "Well you can call me Ray, and you can call me Jay," and you can call ME FAY, and you can call me Jay, but you DOESN'T have to call me Johnson," became their next bonding ritual after their mutual appreciation for the arch.

"You know, Fay, if it wasn't for another famous Ray, there'd be no arch," he pointed out.

She gave him a silly look. "And what a crock, get it?" He looked unsure. "Crock?"

"Heh, heh, heh, Fay, never at a 'Lost,' for words, get it, LOST!" Lost was Fay's maiden name.

"Though I may be lost, at least I haven't yet LOST it."

"I guess you haven't, if you've made it all THIS way. For which you and I should be eternally grateful to this wonderful arch, without the blessed presence of and directional guidance, would never have gotten to this sublime increment in our existence."

"I could drink to that," said Fay, with her right

hand cupped. But now neither of them had anything to drink, though both felt thirst. So after heading over to the Anheuser-Busch company, they bought fresh cups of Budweiser and took a guided tour with the Clydesdales. And so began their involvement.

After they'd spent a few days together, got more acquainted, and exchanged every address and phone number they knew, Fay and Ray embraced and bid each other a tearful farewell at the very site where it all began less than a week earlier, in front of the arch. They agreed to call each other as SOON as they got home, leaving messages with anyone necessary to make SURE the contact was maintained. This was how they'd be able to tell if what they seemed to have was real. After all, if their relationship could survive a mere 3 thousand miles, and a short 3 hour time difference, then there'd surely be something worth trying to maintain. If however, this was merely a case of 2 passing vessels in enlightened transit, then THAT TOO would soon become obvious.

The better part of 2 weeks went by, while Ray and Fay winged their way back across Old Glory, with visions of each other doting out at them everywhere. Suffice it to say, it was a rather sweet haunt for each of them, and a wonderful sign of things to come.

But when Fay found herself riding along what she could have sworn was the Appalachian Trail, and Ray found himself pushing and thumbing across miles upon miles of cactus-laden desert, they both began to think something was wrong. The clincher for Fay was just before she reached the ocean and saw the torch-lady herself dead ahead—but how could it be—the Statue of Liberty? At the same time, Ray found himself on a considerably warmer beach where surfer dudes, duddettes and roller bladers seemed to dominate the scene. So it was truly no surprise they each came to terms with what had happened pretty much at the same time. Call us crazy, but I think we're on the WRONG COAST!

They immediately started calling all the numbers they'd each given the other—Ray found himself in touch with Fay's mom, dad, siblings, several cousins, best friends from high school, etc. Fay got in touch with Ray's family, his friends from high school and college, and a few of his former bosses, including the leasor of his ice cream truck, who assured her Ray could never get lost.

Eventually the confusion became resolved when Fay, who had somehow found herself at Ray's parents' house (and ALL hit it off QUITE well, DESPITE the circumstances) was speaking to Ray over the phone, who was now at the home of Fay's best friend from childhood, Rozzie Lange. And suffice it to say, they had EACH pledged to ALL of their hosts, that EVERY phone bill which had eventually led to this wonderful reunion between the 2 of them would be settled up in full, by the time both of them were able to return to their own respective sides of the continent. And suffice it to say, they were EACH told by everyone concerned not to worry about it.

"Gee, Ray, it looks like we both got a little lost, huh?"

"I thought YOU were the only one of us that was LOST, Fay."

"Yeah, well it doesn't exactly look like YOU'VE found your WAY, Ray, EITHER." They continued to giggle over the irony of the situation involving their last names.

"You know something," Rozz interrupted, from her perch on the stool beside the phone, "if Fay had YOUR last name, you could be rhymin' Ray and Fay once Lost, but now no Way."

As silly as that sounded, it almost made omen-like sense.

"Hey, Fay, did you hear what Rozz just said?" She couldn't, but figured it had to be something sensible. Rozz was a smart girl.

Ray could now hear his father in the background blithering stereotypical California quotes. "Chill OUT, dude! Fer SHIR! Surfs right UP, like ya know like just SO NARLEY COOL, dude!"

"Oh, no, Fay, has he kept doing that to you?" Ronald Way's unusual sense of humor was his prime creativity as an ad exec. And he lived for predicaments like this which gave him the chance to share it.

"Oh, yeah, fer SHIR, DUDE!" Ray moaned and

shook his head.

"What's the matter?" asked Rozz, "aren't they feeding her enough?" Ray felt this had to be the silliest moment of his life.

"Ronald, will you get away from that phone and give this nice young lady a little privacy with our son, please," said Mary Way, as she stood beside her husband with a trayload of snacks. "Care for an appetizer, dear?" Fay looked up and smiled.

"Don't worry, Rozz, they're feeding her plenty." At the moment Ray almost envied Fay her parents' divorced status.

"No, that's okay, Mrs. Way, thanks anyway." Ronald burst out laughing.

"Did you hear that poetry, Mary? I'll bet we could hire her to write jingles for us." At this point, Mary put down the tray, took Ronald by the hand, and pulled him into the kitchen.

"I know," said Rozz, "maybe you guys need some privacy." She left the room, and now they were finally alone to talk.

"Look, Fay, I'm really sorry about my dad's nonsense. It's just that he loves to get a wild rise out of everyone."

"Are you kidding? I love your dad. He's a super guy. And your mom, too. Well, she's a super GAL." Ray liked her response.

"And what do you think of my family? And Rozz?" He knew he could now play around with her a little.

"Well. Well. I guess they're, well, you know, well...."

"Well what? What are you just being a wise guy?"

"They're great. All of them. Your little brother and sister are adorable. And Rozz is kind of how I'd envision a Gypsy fortune teller." He looked around to make sure she was out of the room. Not that he'd meant anything bad, but who knows how that kind of comment could be understood.

"Oh, you mean the way she's always coming up with meaningful phrases, asking hard hitting questions, and often wears her hair under a bandanna?" Could Fay have read his mind?

"And don't forget her crystal ball." They now suddenly found themselves feeling very serious.

"Yeah, and maybe she could peek into it to find out what's happened with us." Ray knew exactly what Fay was getting at.

"Somebody should. Because getting lost like we did is BAD!"

"Boy, I'll say. But it's a good thing both of us had all those numbers and addresses, and people willing to pick us up. After this little hiatus of ours, I'd have been afraid to try to bike anywhere."

"You call what happened to us a little hiatus? I'm telling you, Fay, I think we should seek out professional help. There's no way we could suddenly lose our navigational skills like this without some cause."

"What?   Are you talking about getting THERAPY?"

"You bet your sweet petuti, I am. Otherwise, we may never again be able to go anywhere on our own without something going this wrong. Only the next time we might end up someplace where there's nobody around to help us!" As radical as Ray's proposal sounded, it seemed to make perfect sense.

"But where could we get the therapy? I mean, who could we see? We're both on the other one's end of the country."

If this wasn't ever the perfect excuse for them to reunite where it all began. "What about St. Louis? It worked out GREAT for us the first time."

Fay thought for a minute. "Therapy together in St. Louis? Yeah! My father's a pilot! And my mother's a flight attendant!"

"And my parents have plenty of frequent flier miles coming!"

And so, before one could say East meets West or vice versa it was settled. They each boarded a plane for St. Louis, with Fay having her bike put in storage, hoping whatever had caused their directional screw up could be cured in a hurry. After all, she was STILL in training for the Tour de France, and certainly not even a quirk of THIS magnitude should put a dent in her plans.

Unfortunately for Ray, he had to contend with Fay's parents and her 2 young siblings, as well as one of her youngest cousins on his flight. Fay's

father was the pilot, and her mother the flight
attendant catering to all his needs. And the main
problem here was that this flight had been specially
chartered so there were no other passengers, thus
enabling the hostilities which went with being a
family divided to enter right into Ray's life.

"So, Ray," called Captain Rada Lost, over the
plane's intercom, as they were airborne above
Phoenix, "what are you going to do for my
daughter? You're not going to make the same
mistakes as I did with Laurie, here." Fay's bleached
blonde mother gave him a slight grin and finger
wave from where she stood beside the cockpit door.
In the meantime, Fay's 8-year-old brother, Matthew,
6-year-old sister, Melissa, and 7-year-old cousin,
Monica were pulling his legs, making him feel like a
pair of scissors. "Because we want no more splits in
our family."

"So tell me, Raymond," said Laurie Wencidbin,
"isn't it obvious to you that Fay gets her looks from
ME, and not my hyper ex in the next room, flying
this plane?"

"Hey, I heard that," bellowed Captain Lost, over
the intercom. "You see that, son? You see where
that kind of conceit can land a marriage? Right in
the CRAPPER!" The plane's engines suddenly got
louder, and it felt to Ray like there was some pilot
emotion involved.

"Oh, right, Rada, like you're so humble and
understanding. That's why you had to make SURE

that Fay was still daddy's little girl and would never forget it when she grew up, before you'd even CONSIDER having THESE monsters!"

"VROOOM, I'm DADDY'S BIG MONSTER!" screamed young Matthew in earnest, as he continued to pull on Ray's right leg with all his might. Ray winced as he tried not to react.

"SO WHAT, I'm MOMMY'S BIG MONSTER!" answered Melissa, doing the same to Ray's left leg. Monica was alternating legs with each of them, making sure she got plenty of tugging action on both.

"EEEEEE! I'M A BIG MONSTER, TOO, EEEEEE!" she exclaimed.

After a couple and a half of hours of bickering and battiness which included Captain Lost putting on the autopilot and coming out of the cockpit to argue with Laurie, they finally landed.

"Wow, it's so good to finally be alone again," said Fay, as she rubbed Ray, and sidled him back and forth on the sofa at the boarding house where they were staying.

"Hey, easy there on the legs, Fay; I'm still feeling like a twisted wishbone." He'd already explained the situation to her about her siblings, cousin and parents and she understood completely. However, he still didn't want to complain too much. After all, this was THEIR lives now, and the last thing either of them needed to do was involve the rest of the families any more than necessary.

"I know; I'm sorry. My family's as nutty as your family."

"Nutty? What are you saying? My family's nutty?" Uh, oh, their first fight. Fay wanted to embrace him and make it all better, but knew it might be painful for him. So instead she quickly grabbed the yellow pages and began thumbing through them, looking for the perfect therapist for what they needed in the first place.

"What are you doing, Fay?"

"I'm looking through the yellow pages for the perfect therapist for what we needed in the first place."

"Oh, good idea." Shew! If that wasn't ever a dodged bullet!

Finally the name Rubin Schwartz, T.P.A., caught her fancy

"Good afternoon, Doctor Schwartz's office."

"Hello, is this Rubin Schwartz, Travel Person Assistant?"

There was a brief silence on the other end, as Doctor Schwartz's receptionist tried to make head or tails of that question. "Excuse me?" Jeez, talk about a grand misuse of the phone directory!

"I said is this Doctor Schwartz, the travel guy?"

"Are you feeling all right, miss? You're not on any kind of hallucinogenic drugs, are you?'

"No. I'm in St. Louis, just like you."

"Look, miss, I'm really busy today. What do you want?"

"I want to know if Doctor Schwartz can keep me and my boyfriend from ever getting lost again."

There was another brief silence, as Doctor Schwartz's receptionist was trying to decide whether to hang up on her, or really try to land her as a new patient for the doctor. Finally, she decided to try, figuring she had nothing to lose but another few seconds. "All right, miss, what are you and your boyfriend's names?"

"Lost and Way." Oh my God, why doesn't this girl get a life?

"Look, I'm sorry, miss, I think your problem's a little too complex for the doctor to deal with. Have yourself a great day."

"NO, WAIT! PLEASE, DON'T HANG UP!" The sudden desperate cry in Fay's voice was enough to keep the receptionist hanging on. "Can't Doctor Schwartz help us? I mean the ad said he was a T.P.A." The receptionist had never felt more torn in her life.

"Yes, miss, that's exactly what he is. A THOR-OUGH PSYCHOANALYST. And I don't know how he could help you."

"Because we each got lost going cross-country."

"Here, Fay, let me talk." Ray had just gotten up and Fay handed him the phone. He talked for awhile before he'd done enough explaining to finally get them an appointment. They both knew what a huge hurdle it was they'd cleared.

On the bus ride over to his office, they passed

the arch.

"Ow, wow, Ray, look! This is what brought us to this wonderful impasse!" Some of the other people began to stare at them as they both began getting a little emotional. But it seemed as if so much had happened to them over the past month, they were quite oblivious to the aghast attention.

"After we're done with Doctor Schwartz today, what do you say we head over for a Clydesdale ride and some fresh Bud," said Ray.

"Oh, Ray! Like our first date. You needn't ask me twice. You can call me Fay and you can call me Jay...." Ray quickly joined in.

The receptionist gave them all kinds of looks as they greeted her and filled out the necessary paperwork. This was definitely something new for the textbooks. But Fay and Ray were extremely impressed with Doctor Schwartz's punctuality, and took it as a pretty good sign he'd find the cause of their directional mishap fairly quickly.

"So. You 2 say you left St. Louis together at the same time about 3 and a half weeks ago to return home. Only thing is, you each found yourselves on the wrong ends of the country. Okay, I'm going to ask you to think back very carefully. Back to the EXACT MOMENT before you parted the way at that time. Where were you? And I mean, EXACTLY."

They each thought for a second before answering together.

"In front of the ARCH!" Doctor Schwartz quickly smiled and snapped his finger. If this wasn't ever great.

"Tell me something. Have either of you ever heard of a neurosis called bipolar disorder?" Neither had.

"Well, it sounds to me like you somehow managed to acquire that very peculiar disorder by the symmetrical CURVE of the arch. And what that means is, is that your brains were hypnotized into SUBCONSCIOUSLY SEEING your WORLD DIRECTLY BACKWARDS. And I know that sounds astounding, but much like DYSLEXIA, it CAN HAPPEN."

"But what can we do about it?" asked Fay.

"Simple. Don't ever look at the arch before you leave St. Louis." Fay and Ray suddenly became emotional all over again.

"What do you mean?" pressed Ray. "The arch is the CORNERSTONE of our RELATIONSHIP! We MET there. And there's NO WAY we want to feel like we EVER have to stay away, ANYTIME!" Fay nodded. Doctor Schwartz put his head in his hands. If this wasn't ever a tough caseload! After a moment of thought, he finally came up with what he hoped would be a compromising solution for them.

"All right then. If you have to look at the arch, look at it from a DIFFERENT SIDE INSTEAD." Ray suddenly had a romantic brainstorm.

"FAY!" he said, getting down on one knee.

"Let's try that. We each stand alongside the arch facing North-South instead of East-West. And go off in separate directions until we can't see the arch or each other any longer. And if we can find our way back to each other we'll get MARRIED! Would you DO ME THE HONOR?"

That was 6 months ago. Now they're happily married, living in St. Louis and expect their first child, who'll they'll name Alda Way, regardless of sex. If a girl, the middle name's Blessed, a boy, Bested. And they've many photos to show the child. Ray from the North Pole and Canada, Fay from Mexico and South America.

Wanda
the Jungle Woman

As a small chap, I spent many a year on safari with the grown ups. I learned the thrills and challenges of jungle life, the way most children learn of ABCs, 123s, and DON'T BUG MEs!

My home life consisted primarily of sweeping around the hut, flipping heavy slabs of meat onto and off of our butane grill, and practicing to fire the family rifle in case of trouble. The sounds of lions, tigers, giraffes, hippos, elephants, gazelles and zebras became the music which I grew to know and love.

Suffice it to say, I was weaned in a rather adventurous family, and the visits to our village by the many missionaries assigned to help out the less fortunate in the area was always met by my most curious nature. In my mind, I'd often compare and contrast our lifestyle with theirs. THEY always seemed a tad more civilized than WE, for their purpose for being there was to assist OTHERS to survive—whereas OURS was simply to survive. And it didn't take me long to realize there were those among THEM who were JUST as curious about US.

Sometimes when she'd be out in the brush snooping around, and I'd spot her checking out our supplies, I'd wonder if her plan was to steal them assuming one of the grown ups in HER group had decided to use her as a pawn. My mind always seemed to work that way—like the inbred nature of a boy on safari to stay alert.

But then she'd suddenly up and start darting about, yelling her name and pounding on her chest. "ME, WANDA, JUNGLE GIRL! ME, WANDA, WILD GIRL OF JUNGLE, AW, AWIAWA, AWIAWA!" And then she'd jump around between the trees until any of the grown ups in her group came out of their tent and made her stop.

It was definitely the funnest part of my childhood, bar none, and I always regretted it when they'd make her cut it out. After all, here was a young child perhaps a few years younger than I, with a strong sense of adventure—something I ADMIRED, something I wished I possessed as well. And to a certain extent I DID. But I could never have been that bold or outrageous to let loose with that stuff the way she would. At least I never dared to TRY. Of course, I always found the entertainment she gave me MAGNIFICENT, and even back then I had images of her being in the entertainment industry someday—with lots of people paying her EXCELLENT money to give them the ULTIMATE thrill. I guess I was both rather enterprising for my tender age, as well as IMAGINATIVE. In any case, the fun and ideas I was having has definitely come in handy since then.

When Wanda and I finally got to meet one evening at a family gathering for a feast involving missionaries, hunters and natives alike, I remember hoping she'd fill the night with some antics.

And she didn't disappoint me. When one of the darker natives at our table began chanting an ancient tribal prayer, Wanda began to jump up and down and throw food around—like the effects of the prayer were strictly for MY benefit.

Suffice it to say, this led to quick measures of discipline against both of us—Wanda was promptly removed from the table by her parents, and I was taken back into the hut by my own for breaking out in laughter, lectured harshly by them and no longer permitted to join the group in any form of joint ritual.

"Victor! You're an AWFUL, VILE CHILD! Don't you EVER show such a display AGAIN! Or, you'll be BANISHED from the hut and made to live out there in the jungle, COMPLETELY UNPROTECTED! Is THIS UNDERSTOOD?" my father demanded.

"Yes, your father's RIGHT," resumed my mother. "That girl totally mortified EVERYONE in her MIDST, tonight. And neither your father or I will tolerate ANYTHING you do to CONDONE that HORRIDNESS! Now tomorrow we insist you go over to their tent and THOROUGHLY APOLOGIZE to her mum and pop."

Of course, there was no other answer. I certainly didn't want to have to live out there in the jungle unprotected. Not that I was afraid, mind you, but those MOSQUITOES could be rough. And anyway, when I went over to apologize, I could see Wanda!

And as it turned out, she was QUITE happy to see me. In fact, it was at THAT point I'd begun to realize that my presence had quite an effect on her. "HEY, BIG SPROUT! BIG, BIG SPROUT," she exclaimed as I appeared at the opening of their tent. She danced around beneath the canvas the way a moth would flap about a 60-watt bulb.

"Wanda, CEASE and DESIST!" her father yelled. "This is NOT the way we conduct ourselves before a visitor!" She slowed down to a tap step, but kept the giggle alive. GAWD, she was SUPERB! The way she showed no intimidation. Even at that age, she was beginning to drive me wild.

"Just ignore her," her mother said to me. "The jungle's obviously become quite an influence. Expect it'll be FRONT and CENTER in her MEMOIRS, someday."

Of course, I had all I could do to keep from breaking up all over again, as I had on the previous evening. Yet it was quickly becoming obvious to me that Wanda's parents were not the LEAST bit offended by my response to her behavior.

"So, what can we do for you, young man?" resumed her mother, after I'd finally managed to hold a straight face.

Suddenly, I had the greatest idea of my LIFE to that point. Because it led me to make the BOLDEST MOVE to that point. "MY folks thought it would be quite lovely it I were to take Wanda for an adventurous sightseeing stroll." Her parents looked at each other with doubt. "Oh, it's perfectly safe, see? I've got me the rifle for protection. And it's loaded. And I'm quite well briefed in how to use it, you know," I assured them, lifting it above my shoulders.

Naturally, out there on safari you never went anywhere without the loaded weapon. It could be way too dangerous.

Wanda wasted NO time in pleading her case. "Oh, PLEASE, mummy, PLEASE, PLEASE, POPPY, can I PLEASE GO with 'im? I WON'T get into any TROUBLE, HONEST!" I guess her pouting little eyes must have done the rest.

"Well, Herbert, I really don't see the harm in it." Ruth looked at him like she was trying to convey that it would be the best thing for all concerned — it would get Wanda out of their hair, and give her the chance to become more acquainted with others — both ends to very important means to them.

"Oh, I guess it's okay if mum says so; SHE'S the boss."

"Oh, THANK YOU, MUM AND POP! THANK YOU just SO MUCH!" Wanda gave them both great big hugs, and suffice it to say I now felt ready for ANYTHING!

"Don't worry, I'll take QUITE GOOD CARE of her," I said.

Now obviously I'm sure you folks don't REALLY want to know what a DEEPLY AROUSED 15-year-old boy would do with an obviously SIMILARLY aroused 12-and-1/2-year-old GIRL, out in the lush brush of Africa's DARKEST AREAS. And if the somewhat SUGGESTIVE ADVERBS and ADJECTIVES in that last sentence doesn't give it away, then I STRONGLY suggest you read it OVER to yourself again VERY CAREFULLY! God knows, I'VE been doing that ever SINCE!

In any case, she DIDN'T get pregnant, and it was of course, NO BIG DEAL. It just became a WONDERFUL memory for EACH of us, as well as the OPPORTUNITY to FULFILL our adolescence, the way MANY others only WISH they could.

Of course, if Wanda's family hadn't moved back to good ole Londontown within the next few weeks, this story might NOT have turned out as lucky for us as it has to this point. Because although we both knew there were risks of our promiscuity being exposed, I don't think that would have stopped us from keeping it up. And I don't even want to THINK about the possible consequences which could have RESULTED.

But who would have thought that fate would actually have been KIND enough to bring Wanda and I together again, some 5 years later! It happened back in the big city, after both our families had settled into the more relaxed and conservative type of lives.

I was listening in earnest to my new police scanner one evening — the most perfect way to find out about all the big stuff taking place around town. Suddenly I heard the constables conferring about a rather strange young lady, who was right then in the process of scaling one of London's TALLEST BUILDINGS! And naturally, there was quite a bit of CONCERN among the force, as it wasn't clear whether this was a possible suicide attempt, or a most ATTENTIVE way to train for the next "Everest Venture." In either case I'm sure it would have made Sir Hillary DANG PROUD! But I immediately knew that regardless of the motives for this action, the young lady in question was putting her life in the hands of the DEVIL!

And the funny thing was, that at that very MOMENT, I'd been in a state of the FONDNESS of REMINISCE over Wanda—in the most PHYSICAL sense as well—AH HEM! Upon hearing the broadcast, and the girl's description, the alarm of the moment had set in when it seemed as if these were the EXACT FEATURES of my WANDA being spoken of, and BIT by AGONIZING BIT, the realization piled itself upon my SOUL, like the AWFUL FEELINGS Sherlock Holmes would have incurred, were it to slowly but SURELY become obvious to him his DEAR WATSON was in ACTUALITY the culprit to an EXTREMELY HEINOUS CRIME! In ANY case, I knew there wasn't a MOMENT to lose to ACT.

So after dashing outside to my motor scooter as quickly as I could, I fired up and gunned it the way I might begin a universal race to the stars. I knew I hadn't a second to lose, because if this was in fact, my Wanda, then based on every single past experience I'd ever had with her, there'd be NOTHING I could say to her which she'd NOT respond to. In other words, if that were really her upon the building, then nobody but nobody would have a better chance of talking her down safely than I. And of course, this would also make me quite the HERO, although this type of recognition I needed NOT in order to assure me any ego inflation.

After cutting, bucking and weaving through the traffic with all the Knievel-like moves of the Evil One himself, I soon found myself at the building just before Trafalgar Square where she was located in tight clutch of a mid-widthed rope, which she had somehow managed to attach around a scaffold beside the building. And suffice it to say, she was in a fairly high elevated state at that moment—almost 10 stories up I'd say—making me realize how much I truly had my work cut out for me. And I knew that if I were to talk her down, it could be MOST precarious. Of course, if I were able to get her to cooperate with the authorities, so that she'd go down willingly with them on their ladders, that'd be FINE. What it depended on, I knew, was what her INTENTIONS were.

I knew I could find those out right away. After grabbing one of the constables' bullhorns, I let loose with a cry of "WANDA!"

"I beg your pardon, young man, this is a CONSTABULARY AFFAIR you happen to be interfering with! Do you have any IDEA how SERIOUS an OFFENSE THAT IS?"

I ignored the constable as long as I could, until Wanda let me know she knew I was standing there. "Oh, VICTOR! Whatever are you DOING HERE, LET ME SEE YOU, you SCOUNDREL!"

"WANDA, TAKE IT EASY! STAY PERFECTLY STILL, AND LET ONE OF THE CONSTABLES BRING YOU DOWN UPON THE LADDER! OKAY?" She obeyed me to the LETTER, staring down at me with that special fondness and affection which had existed between us years earlier.

"Young man, you should receive a medal for this," said the same constable who was ready to arrest me only moments earlier, as Wanda was brought safely to earth.

And suffice it say, she looked hotter than ever. In fact, if my trousers were any TIGHTER, I'm sure I'd have incurred a most painful state of PRIAPISM at that moment. Turns out she WAS just trying to get herself some attention, the kind that frustrated people often need to get, in order to reassure themselves of their actual state of aliveness. But after seeing ME, that was all taken care of in FULL.

As we rode my motor scooter back through town, I couldn't help but notice all the guys giving her ogling looks all about, as we caught up with each other's news. As it turns out, her life was at LEAST as boring as MINE. She'd just finished with school, had no skills, or any idea of what she wanted to DO with her life. In fact, she informed me, in attempting to scale that building, her belief was she'd found she was truly qualified to become an acrobat in the circus, now that her fear of heights was dissolved — and she wondered if I was interested in joining it WITH her. Of course, I had neither knowledge nor desires of or for THAT kind of life — I believed MYSELF more qualified for something along the lines of an administrative supervisor, if only I could find something in such a profession which could earn ME some cash. And it wasn't after being with her much longer, and enjoying the carnal ecstasy she provided like never before, when I suddenly REALIZED EXACTLY what could not ONLY give us EACH the types of positions we sought, but would keep us together as a TEAM. And granted there were some RISKS involved, yet it was quite obvious to THAT point we both LIVED for TAKING them. And so, our arrangement's proven marvelous to now, we've taken every necessary precaution, business is BOOMING, and Wanda always does the chaps SO WELL! Suffice it to say, it's been a great year.

Cafeteria Spontaneity

The dayroom activities were in full swing. Ephram was making like he was blowing away all his fellow patients with a machine gun. Ralph and Boris pretended to die, but then Boris would do gorilla imitations while Ralph picked his nose; then made like he was drawing something in the air with the mucous. Terry was making train noises and marching back and forth like he was one, while Saul just sort of continued sitting there in his meditative state of silence. Of course, in his own ironic way, HE was the one in charge. He spoke so RARELY, that on ANY occasion when he DID, everyone ELSE in the room would immediately STOP what they were doing and gather at his feet.

It seemed to be a sound, working arrangement which formed the long-going bond between these 5 men, and quite frankly it would be anything but HONEST to say that they hadn't mastered LIFE, in their own INIMITABLE way. Of course, even so, their individual cases were always being discussed and HARPED upon by all of their CARETAKERS at the institution, if for nothing MORE than to TRY to figure out WHY each ONE had ended UP here, and exactly what TYPES of situations render people like this. It made for the most GRANT MONEY SPENT for RESEARCH in the institution, and while it would be anyone's GUESS, WHY these lifestyles were less APPRECIATED than MOST, it provided the INSTITUTION FOUNDATION and VALIDITY.

Through the glass partition which separated the dayroom from the cafeteria, waves of sunshine reflected the moving shadows of those INTELLECTS employed at the institution who were in the process of having their lunch while they basically discussed the progress, or lack thereof of the status quo of PATIENTS in their care. And of course, the contrasts in styles between the SOCIAL WORKERS, MEDICAL PROFESSIONALS, SECURITY PEOPLE and even the DIETITIANS, COOKS and KITCHEN PEOPLE GELLED in the SAME kind of HARMONIOUS WAVES as did the people in the dayroom as they ALL continued carrying on with their daily routines—EACH group of people at least in

APPEARANCE seeming to have built up a VISUAL OBLIVION to those of the OTHERS in the room that ADJOINED THEIRS.

And this was TYPICAL and ORDERLY, as it made for the SMOOTH conductivity of the PROGRESS of EVERYONE at the institution. AS in EVERY type of COMMUNITY which included MANY walks of life, the EFFICIENCY of the ENTIRE UNIT depended on the ROUTINES of EVERY PERSON in the ESTABLISHMENT being UPHELD and MAIN-TAINED without FLAW, and of COURSE were there EVER a CHANCE that SOMEONE would SUD-DENLY act OUTSIDE of HIS or HER ROUTINE, and CEASE the NORMAL and ESTABLISHED PATTERNS of HIS or HER POSITION, THEN you PRETTY much had a VERY STRONG CHANCE of COMPLETE CHAOS IMMEDIATELY being the NORM. And FORTUNATELY, up to NOW, THIS had NOT OCCURRED here.

Doctor Kessler sprinkled dressing on his salad while Doctor Rodenbush sipped his ice tea. "You know, Arnie," said Doctor Rodenbush, "I have a theory about Mr. Ephram's behavior that I'm considering submitting to the board."

Doctor Kessler appeared quite enthused as he chewed. "Does it have something to do with battle fatigue?" he asked, in his medically assertive manner. "Because we're all quite aware of how VETERANS on the front line of battle feel so DEPRESSED about it being OVER, that they tend to HALLUCINATE that it's still HAPPENING simply to give them a sense of their OWN WORTH."

"Well, THAT'S the STANDARD theory in our profession, Arnie, but the PARTICULAR theory I have is based on Mr. Ephram's HOME life, BEFORE he went OFF to war." Doctor Kessler appeared quite surprised.

"You don't SAY, George. So YOU believe that Mr. Ephram's tendency to like to pretend he's killing his fellow PATIENTS stems from a hostile HOME environment." Doctor Rodenbush nodded.

Nurse Mackenzie looked up from her bean chili to acknowledge them. "You know, that seems to make a lot of SENSE, Arnie. I mean WHY is it that WE in the MEDICAL profession always ASSUME that our VETERAN patients are always screwed up due to WAR. And at the SAME time, say that patients like Saul, who are at the OTHER end of the spectrum to the extent that they're always so SUBDUED, automatically MEANS that THEY had such an INTIMIDATING home life, they're AFRAID to even be NOTICED. When in FACT, there's a REAL GOOD CHANCE that THEY simply have NEVER had ANY type of MOTIVATION at all."

"You know, Maura's RIGHT," interjected Larry Brett, a social worker with a PHD in behavioral science. "One of the COOKS over there has a SISTER she was telling me about who likes PRETENDING to be different ANIMALS. And SHE believes it was SIMPLY because she found her GERBILS

FASCINATING, not because there was any kind of REPRESSED HOSTILITY which needed to be LET OUT."

"Well, GEE, Larry," said Doctor Kessler, "in all FAIRNESS to that CHEF, what has her SISTER to do with any of the PATIENTS in HERE?" Larry had a pretty clear cut answer to THAT question.

"In case you hadn't NOTICED, Arnie, most of our PATIENTS like to PRETEND they're things. So MAYBE we could apply THAT theory to MOST if not ALL of THEM!" Doctor Kessler thought for a moment and then nodded. The discussion continued becoming more INTUITIVE and began to FLOURISH among many OTHER staff members who were in the cafeteria. Of course this was basically the daily routine of every one of them, who spent many a moment LUNCHING and SHARING ideas and theories like their jobs DEPENDED on it.

Saul had suddenly made a high buzzing sound, while all the other patients in the dayroom immediately froze and dropped to the floor. After all, this was the FIRST PEEP out of him in a good 3 weeks, and the others KNEW this meant there was some VERY IMPORTANT INSIGHT about to be SHARED with them. Saul continued to hum as he kept getting louder. This was something BIG and everyone around him KNEW it.

Nurse Mackenzie suddenly felt a PING against her FOREHEAD, as one of the BEANS in her chili had flipped up and HIT her. Of course, she had no IDEA this was SO, and IMMEDIATELY assumed something ELSE. "Really, Arnie, just because you don't AGREE with our THEORY, doesn't mean you have to start BEHAVING like one of the PATIENTS!"

"What the HELL are you TALKING about, Maura?" demanded Doctor Kessler, in a manner which Nurse Mackenzie not ONLY felt was BELLIGERENT, but one which SUGGESTED she was BEING RIDICULED.

"I'm talking about THIS," she said, taking Doctor Kessler's salad and THROWING it in his face. Before LONG a food fight had ERUPTED, while the 5 in the dayroom watched in amusement.

"Now who's crazy?" said Saul to the others. "It took me 3 weeks CONCENTRATION to move that BEAN." They congratulated him.

"You 'da MAN!" Ephram said finally. "You REALLY 'da man."

Vestiges of Vagrancy

Out in the street, the forlorn and haggard down-and-outers occupied the space like slithering moles. If there was some kind of SELECTION process which ENABLED ANY ONE of them to find RELIEF from their DREGS, the TIME for it could NOT have been RIGHTER.

The early winter wind had picked up with a fierce intensity, and the coating of snow which had begun to fall had become grey, slippery ice within the past few hours. Yet sometimes the WORST WEATHER could be a RADICAL CAMOUFLAGE for an AMAZING TURNABOUT of LUCK.

After all, this was the HOLIDAY season — the time where all were supposed to put AWAY their indifference to others — to HELP the downtrodden and less fortunate. And although this HADN'T been the INTENTION of one Leopold LaLonde, as his LIMOUSINE passed FASTIDIOUSLY through the NEIGHBORHOOD, due to the MERE NEGLIGENCE of his CHAUFFEUR as well as the EVER DECREASING VISIBILITY, THIS would be a DAY which would change not only HIS life, but the life of one of THIS neighborhood's POOREST waifs.

"MY GOD, Hawkins," he said to his CHAUF-FEUR, as they passed some loosely boarded up buildings which used to be a tavern, a bakery and a dry cleaner, "I thought you KNEW your way AROUND! If you wanted me BUMPED OFF, why didn't you just tell my BUTLER?"

"With all due RESPECT, sir, I don't feel too safe, MYSELF."

"You know, Hawkins, during my EARLIER years as a FILM critic, I'd seen MANY FILMS with HORRORS as LOATHSOME as this. Yet in my WORST NIGHTMARES, I'd have NEVER POSSIBLY IMAGINED such decrepitude. How the HELL did you wind us up HERE? I SWEAR to you, Hawkins, if we SURVIVE this night, YOU'D BETTER KNOW, I'll be SEEING TO it that YOU take a SPECIAL SEMINAR on the city's GEOGRAPHY!"   Hawkins noted the panic in Leopold's voice, and tried his best to conceal his amusement.

"Something FUNNY, Hawkins?" So far things were NOT going as planned.

"Well, sir," he said, with the intent to offset the tension by forming the NEXT scenario as CAREFULLY as he COULD, "it's JUST that I don't BELIEVE there are GEOGRAPHY seminars given on the PROS and CONS of the city's BEST and WORST neighborhoods." Hawkins gazed at Leopold in the rear-view mirror to see if his expression had uplifted a bit. It HADN'T. "Of course, it WOULD be a FINE IDEA, sir." By now Hawkins was able to keep a straight face. But by the time they reached the next stop light, even HE had trouble not grimacing.

"HOLY JESSUP!, Hawkins!   I don't suppose you'd considered RUNNING it. I mean, after all, it's only our LIVES that are at stake here." Hawkins was NOW sure he'd been made QUITE the fool.

But SUDDENLY the knocking at the window came JUST before the light turned green. "Hey, POPS! Open up. I'm YOURS, doll. I'll do you ANY WAY YOU WANT! FREE of CHARGE! Hey, it ain't EVERY day a SWEET LIMO like THIS comes through THIS neighborhood."

Hawkins dropped the back window a crack,

JUST so Leopold could SEE her, although his MOTIVES were quite DISGUISED. Yet he felt SURE ENOUGH that when Leopold saw her, he'd suddenly FORGET where he was, or at LEAST to the extent where he wouldn't turn her AWAY. "What's THIS, sir? It appears as though there's a DAMSEL in DISTRESS attempting to grab your ATTENTION. At the very LEAST!" By NOW the light had turned green. "But perhaps we should be OFF now."

"No, Hawkins! DON'T YOU GO ANYWHERE! Well, pull the car over to the CURB, man. Perhaps I can do SOMETHING to accommodate her. After all, this IS the holiday season. That special time of year when we're supposed to HELP our fellow MAN."

"Well in case you hadn't NOTICED, sir," said Hawkins as he JOYFULLY pulled the limo over, "THIS is NOT a man."

Leopold looked out at the young woman with a SHARP, OGLING glance. "You've got THAT right, Hawkins. Now roll down the window. ALL the way!" Hawkins was more than pleased to comply.

"So young lady," began Leopold, "what brings you out here?"

"Guess you could say I'm looking to make myself a LOVE connection. You?"

Leopold suddenly felt QUITE AWKWARD, being that he'd NEVER found himself in this POSITION before. Of course, this girl seemed as INTERESTED in him, as ANY he'd ever KNOWN in his 47 years, and this was NO time for him to start worrying about a reputation, when there was really NOBODY OUT there that cared if he HAD one or NOT!

"Well let's just say, young lady, that my CHAUFFEUR here has QUITE a JUTTING sense of direction." He gave Hawkins a slight wink in the rear-view mirror.

"Coming right back at you, sir," said Hawkins, feeling as PLEASED with himself, as he'd ever felt since he'd been in the employ of Leopold.

"So, miss. What might your NAME be?" resumed Leopold.

"Candy. Candy McDandy." Suddenly Leopold sensed something wasn't quite right.

"You know what, miss? I sense something ISN'T QUITE RIGHT!"

She looked at Hawkins in dismay, as they were NOW secretly at ODDS about how to HANDLE Leopold.

After a moment she said, "tell you what, pops. You put me up at your PAD, take care of all my NEEDS 'til my DYING DAY, which I KNOW you can DO since you're OBVIOUSLY fuckin' LOADED, and I'll take care of all YOUR needs 'til YOUR dying day. Now does THAT MAKE THINGS QUITE RIGHT, HUH, POPS?"

Leopold finally cracked a smile, which quickly became a giggle, then a hearty laugh. "You know something, miss? I just have ONE thing to say. WHERE THE FUCK HAVE YOU BEEN ALL MY

LIFE?"

And so Candy McDandy moved in with Leopold and his staff, and there was PLENTY of ROOM for her on the estate, in his LIFE and for whatever kinds of SPONTANEOUS WHIMS she had. And she HAD LOTS of THOSE, which Leopold was QUITE READY to MEET. When she wanted new CLOTHES, he bought her the most EXPENSIVE in the WORLD. When she wanted a car, he gave her a brand new Rolls-Royce. When she felt the need to go even FURTHER around her NEW FREE WORLD, he took her to Paris, Zurich, Milan, etc. And when she wanted to get HIGH, Leopold CONTACTED the most ACCOMMODATING DRUG LORDS in the world, who were MORE than HAPPY to come VISIT her at his estate with ANYTHING THEY could PROVIDE for her. And of COURSE, when she wanted to hear MUSIC or see MOVIES, Leopold brought her BACKSTAGE to CONCERTS of her CHOICE, as well as bringing her to Hollywood to mingle with STARS on MOVIE sets. And FORTUNATELY there was STILL plenty of MONEY left to his STAFF which they received after Leopold and Candy had died of AIDS, which they ALL knew SHE had, along with a GREAT last few months, and THEIR FUTURES ASSURED.

Bubble in the Juice

I magine, if you WILL, life WAY in the future. OR, perhaps in a PARALLEL UNIVERSE. OR, perhaps just in MY imagination.

Well you see, THAT'S the GREAT THING about THIS PARTICULAR STORY! You as the READER, have the CHOICE of PRETENDING WHETHER THIS is a STORY from FAR in the FUTURE, a PARALLEL UNIVERSE, or JUST ANOTHER FARCE from MY WACKY IMAGINATION.

Now of COURSE, you KNOW that THIRD thing is TRUE. But if I can HYPE the STORY up SO MUCH MORE, by giving YOU the READER the CHANCE to STIMULATE your BRAIN SO MUCH MORE by BEING ABLE TO READ this story, and DECIDE whether it TAKES PLACE WAY in the FUTURE, OR a PARALLEL UNIVERSE, as WELL as JUST in my GREAT IMAGINATION, then YOU'D BEST BE BELIEVING IT'S a PRETTY AMAZING STORY and the BEST PART of it's CERTAINLY YET TO COME! And it IS!

OKAY, then. So NOW that I'm DONE with all that EARLY STORY HYPE, and YOU the READERS like TOTALLY DROOLING in ANTICIPATION for MORE, then I GUESS this would be a GREAT time to GIVE you JUST THAT. MORE that is. And by that, I DON'T mean that BRAND of CIGARETTE. Of course, if you're someone you SMOKES when you READ and you SIMPLY FORGOT to LIGHT up THIS time, then by GOLLY, FEEL FREE to go GRAB yourself a BUTT. Or HER BUTT! Or ANY BUTT you CHOOSE. But JUST KNOW that THIS STORY'S ACTUALLY about YOUR HEALTH and WELL-BEING, and you may want to consider THAT FIRST!

NOW! Do you know ANYTHING at ALL about SCIENCE? THOUGHT not. Me EITHER. What about MEDICINE? THOUGHT not. Me EITHER. At least not ME, THE WRITER of THIS STORY. However, ME, the CHARACTER in this story knows LOTS about BOTH! And is INCLINED to UTILIZE it as COMPLETELY as POSSIBLE for the BENEFIT of HUMANITY. Well, I guess THAT'S a BIT of an EXAGGERATION. No ACTUALLY, that's a HU-MUNGUS exaggeration. I could care LESS about humanity. Well actually I DO care, but I care MORE about MAKING GOOD MONEY. And I ALSO CARE about the PEOPLE who buy the FRUIT juices from the COMPANY I WORK for. Well, actually I CARE about THEIR well-being. Well I care about their MONEY. Of course, WITHOUT their WELL-BEING, they'd HAVE no MONEY to SPEND on JUICE. So I GUESS you could SAY that I CARE about their WELL-BEING enough to want their MONEY. THERE! Finally, the most HONEST PHRASE in this PARAGRAPH. And with THAT I'll NOW begin a NEW one.

In my PROFESSION, I'm a SCIENTIST, IN-VENTOR and ENTREPRENEUR SUPREME. While my responsibilities may seem MINISCULE to those who consume my company's JUICE drinks, the FACT that I've been ABLE to do my JOB so WELL is the REASON this is SO. In OTHER words, it's MY COMPLETE TASK at HAND to make ABSOLUTELY CERTAIN my company's JUICE drinks are SAFE to DRINK. I POSSESS the BURDEN to make ABSOLUTELY SURE there are no DANGEROUS ELEMENTS IN them.

With me so far? COOL! NOW! Let me ASK you something. You don't have to ANSWER of COURSE, since how COULD you. So just answer for YOUR-SELF, for your OWN benefit. I THINK you can DO that. Good. Okay then. When YOU, (though THIS PARTICULAR SITUATION is MORE applicable if you're a JUICE drinker for MY analysis, BUT as a CONSUMER of ANY product, which I'M SURE YOU ARE, even if JUICE makes you SICK) go OUT and PURCHASE something, SPEND YOUR MONEY on ANYTHING for the BETTERMENT of your LIFE, or EVEN for the WORSENING of your LIFE, such as CIGARETTES which I INDICATED EARLIER in the STORY, do YOU take NOTE of the product's COMPONENTS? In OTHER words, do YOU read LABELS for INGREDIENTS or if there are NO labels, INQUIRE about the MAKE UP of the PRODUCT in QUESTION? I MEAN, like for INSTANCE, if you go into a CLOTHING store to buy a SWEATER which MAY or may NOT be LINED with WOOL, but you KNOW for a FACT WOOL makes you ITCH like the DICKENS as it DOES ME, are you GOING to ASK the SALESPERSON if there's wool IN the SWEATER, even if you don't SEE any just to make SURE, or if you go into a FURNITURE store to buy a SOFA but don't WANT there to be ANY LEATHER in it because leather can feel COLD against your BODY, or you CARE about ANIMAL RIGHTS like I do, would you ASK the salesperson if there WAS in fact LEATHER in the SOFA, assuming you weren't SURE? I ASSUME the ANSWER'S YES.

NOW. In ALL products, at LEAST in YOUR world and time (as you MIGHT RECALL I INDICATED BEFORE in the STORY how THIS STORY could be TAKING PLACE in the FAR FUTURE or a DISTANT UNIVERSE, or SIMPLY my OWN IMAGINATION, and of course, the REASON I'm now REMINDING you of THIS, is because I'm ABOUT to INDICATE the PART of the STORY which sets it APART from YOUR world), but as I was ALSO ABOUT TO remind you, ALL PRODUCTS, in BOTH YOUR world and MY WORLD of THIS STORY, are REQUIRED by LAW to POST ANY POSSIBLY HAZARDOUS INGREDIENTS and/or MATERIALS in their MAKE UP, so that the GENERAL PUBLIC is AWARE of what RISKS they may INCUR by the USE of such PRODUCTS.

But what I'VE done, is taken the PROCEDURE of PRODUCT SCRUTINY a FEW STEPS FURTHER than ANYTHING YOU KNOW of in YOUR WORLD and TIME. The CLOSEST PROCEDURE in ANY SCIENCE FICTION STORY YOU might KNOW to what I'VE

done, and DO REGULARLY, would be a VERY
CLEVER MOVIE about a SURGERY being done on
an IMPORTANT POLITICIAN by a TEAM of
PHYSICIANS and SCIENTISTS who were SHRUNK
DOWN to MOLECULAR size and INJECTED into his
BODY. By the way, did they SAVE the guy? I
THINK I FELL ASLEEP before I FINISHED
WATCHING the flick. But it was STILL a GREAT
FLICK and an INSPIRATION to ME! Because THAT'S
how I INSPECT all our JUICES. I'm SHRUNK into
this TINY BUBBLE and DROPPED in for a LOOKSY!

And of COURSE, the BUBBLE ITSELF is STRONG
enough to withstand ANY type of PRESSURE. It's as
they say, INVINCIBLE! So once it's REMOVED
from the JUICE, and I'VE MADE my COMPLETE
ANALYSIS, and DECIDED WHETHER or not the
JUICE is COMPLETELY SAFE to DRINK and SELL,
the BUBBLE and MYSELF are RETURNED to normal
SIZE and I go HOME for the DAY! Pretty CLEVER,
HUH? And I INVENTED it! What's THAT? You
thought I meant I WAS the BUBBLE? Oh, are you
GONNA GET YOURS! So THAT'S PRETTY MUCH
my story in a NUTSHELL. Or a BUBBLE!

However, one of the GREAT PROVERBS of
STORY crafting is that THERE'S NO TIME like the
PRESENT. And even in MY WORLD of this GREAT
STORY, we've STILL not managed to COMPLETELY
VANQUISH INCOMPETENCE. You know. PEOPLE
who don't THINK before they ACT. See we got this
guy, Monahan, here at the company, whose a total

IDIOT. So NATURALLY he's in SALES. In fact, he's in the ROOM with me RIGHT NOW! If ONLY he could HEAR what I'm SAYING to him! Oh, don't WORRY, HE WILL. He'll MOST DEFINITELY be getting a PIECE of MY MIND VERY SOON! Along with his SEVERANCE pay. You see, Monahan LOVES our JUICE. That's probably why he's so GOOD in SALES. But UNFORTUNATELY he can't READ very well. Like when the JUICE I'M IN is in the vial labeled TESTING, and he's NOW SUCKING IT DOWN! With any luck, it'll be SOUR, he'll spit it OUT and it'll be SAFE for me to regrow. Otherwise it's the WHOLE SEWER SYSTEM FIRST!

Lamp of Love

W illis was a man of the world. Well, KIND of. He'd LOVE to ride his MOPED around town to show off, and sometimes when he was feeling REALLY adventurous, he'd even ride it OUT of town. And on days when he felt REALLY cool he'd sometimes ride it out of STATE. Of course, THAT could be a most BUMPY ride, since he was AFRAID to ride it on the HIGHWAY. Which proved that aside from being COOL he was also INTELLIGENT. Especially, since it only WENT 12 miles per hour. But his really cool CAREER enabled him to travel with it all OVER. What was that? Why he was a NEWSPAPER carrier.

And he ALSO had a thing for YARD sales and FLEA markets. Which meant that ALONG with his great CAREER, he ALSO had a great BUSINESS sense. He KNEW the value of a BROKEN TABLE or a PAPERBACK BOOK with a TORN COVER. He got SO NOTICED when on days he had ACTUALLY had his PAPER route FINISHED, and STILL plenty of papers LEFT in his PORTABASKET, he'd stop and buy ALL the JUNK he could STILL pack IN there. Of course, his MOMMY and DADDY thought he was a PACK rat. They didn't SEE their son's COLLECTIONS as a PROMISING LIFESTYLE. In fact, THEY thought their SON was KIND of a LOSER. But at 52, he was the ONLY one of the 3 of them that could REALLY GET AROUND. So they put UP with his CLUTTERING WAYS JUST so THEY could have all their PHYSICAL NEEDS met. It worked out GOOD for ALL of them.

And if nothing ELSE, at least WILLIS, unlike their OTHER offsprings was OKAY to take CARE of his MOMMY and DADDY. Because while Willis' brothers and sisters had REAL careers and REAL lives, they had basically taken THEIR love from mommy and daddy and WIPED their ASSHOLES with it. They had no TIME to bother or come a CALLING. Hey, BESIDES, let Willis deal with THEIR needs—he had NO OTHER QUALIFICATIONS ANY-HOW; that was THEIR attitude.

Of course, Willis' mommy and daddy always WISHED that Willis would someday get married and give them some nice GRANDKIDS to play with and SPOIL. Yet they ALSO knew the chances of THAT happening were about the SAME as the POPE joining a VIOLENT STREET gang. Willis and WOMEN mixed like CHOCOLATE and BATTERY acid, ICE CREAM and NAPALM, TRAINS and AVALANCHES... well I THINK you see where I'm GOING with this.

Naturally, Willis' mommy and daddy STILL always TRIED to fix Willis UP, whenever they thought there MIGHT be the SLIGHTEST SLIVER of HOPE for ROMANCE. Like his MOMMY LOVED to play Mah-Jong and ONE of the LADIES she PLAYED with had a 45-year-old DAUGHTER with 3 children, who'd been INVOLVED in a BITTER DIVORCE, but was NOW READY to try her luck in the DATING pool again, after FINALLY coming to the CONCLUSION that NO man was as BIG a DICK as her EX! So NATURALLY this would HAVE to include Willis, since EVERYONE that KNEW Willis SWORE he was and always HAD been just the SWEETEST BOY! And how could it NOT work out, since this woman's MOTHER played Mah-Jong 3 times a WEEK with Willis' MOMMY. So they TRIED it. UNFORTUNATELY, it turned out that Willis was MUCH MORE INTERESTED in playing with that woman's 3 CHILDREN than he was in being with the WOMAN. And suffice it to say, this led to QUITE A FEW COMMENTS between ALL the ladies in Willis' MOMMY'S Mah-Jong group about how Willis was so JUVENILE and RETARDED-LIKE that it was SO IMPORTANT that Willis' DADDY had enough in his RETIREMENT fund to TAKE CARE of Willis someday when he became too OLD to wipe his own ASS. Which, FORTUNATELY he DID, so THAT would be all SET. But in all fairness to Willis, the DAUGHTER of the LADY in Willis' MOMMY'S Mah-Jong group they tried to fix him UP with was a FAT, UGLY, WRINKLED PRUNE. So THERE!

And Willis' DADDY was ALWAYS reading the SINGLES page of his NEWSPAPER which he always got for FREE since he'd been one of the PAPER'S TOP REPORTERS in his day. Of course, anyone who GOT that paper got THAT SINGLES section for free. I ONLY MENTIONED it as an IRRELEVANT POINT because I NEEDED to fill my QUOTA of WORDS in this STORY. And I thought it sounded INTEREST-ING, but looking BACK on it NOW, it WASN'T. But ANYWAY, this DIDN'T HELP Willis.

So Willis simply kept going ON with his life, which was GOOD supposedly since it wasn't DEATH. And in his own WAY, he lived up to his OWN expectations, and when it came right DOWN to it, who ELSE'S did he need to live up to?

And one day after Willis had finished his paper route, he happened by a nice yard sale in the neighborhood. Naturally, the people RUNNING it KNEW they were about to make a small FORTUNE!

In fact, it had gotten to the POINT where MANY of the people in Willis' neighborhood were now FEUDING with his MOMMY and DADDY, over the YARD SALES which they held CONSTANTLY, enabling Willis to bring MORE NEEDLESS CRAP into their DAMN HOUSE! And of COURSE, the neighbors COMPLETELY DENIED they kept HOLDING their yard sales because of the PROFIT-ABILITY of having Willis in the area. However, YOU and I both KNOW THOSE PEOPLE'S CLAIMS were ALSO a bunch of NEEDLESS CRAP!

ANYWAY, on this PARTICULAR day, Willis actually DID something at this YARD sale he'd NEVER done at either a YARD sale or a FLEA market in his ENTIRE LIFE! He BOUGHT ONLY ONE THING. A RUSTY OLD TABLE lamp, which had ACTUALLY caught his EYE from PRACTICALLY a HALF-MILE AWAY. And while the people who HELD this yard sale were PRIVATELY PRETTY P.O.-ED at Willis for ONLY BUYING ONE THING, Willis had FELT SOMETHING about that LAMP which he'd NEVER FELT before.

AS SHABBY as the lamp LOOKED, Willis ACTUALLY SENSED there MIGHT have been something MAGIC about it, yet he had no idea WHAT NOR did he SHARE this belief about the lamp with ANYONE.

Which WAS in fact, something ELSE which set Willis apart from MANY. He'd OFTEN GET WEIRD HUNCHES about things, and he'd NEVER TELL anyone, so NOBODY in his LIFE ever KNEW he HAD those kinds of HUNCHES. So I GUESS, in THAT sense, THIS CONFIRMS what I WROTE about Willis at the BEGINNING of the STORY, about him being COOL.

So he BOUGHT the lamp, and left the people GRUMBLING, and WONDERING if they shouldn't ever have another YARD sale, or warn the OTHER neighbors that Willis was in FACT CURED of his TENDENCY to SPEND SO MUCH MONEY at ANY ONE SALE. He THEN brought it home for his MOMMY and DADDY to see. And they were SO HAPPY this was ALL he'd bought that day, they ACTUALLY PUT IT GLEEFULLY on their LIVING room TABLE. And Willis knew that late at NIGHT after his mommy and daddy went to bed, he'd have SO MUCH FUN using the LIGHT from the lamp to read his COMIC books with. But what he DIDN'T know was the LAMP REALLY WAS MAGIC. And what it DID was MAKE WOMEN HORNY when it was ON. The PROBLEM was, when Willis called Domino's later and ordered a PIZZA, the REAL SEXY WOMAN who DELIVERED it was ALL OVER him. Until she asked him to turn off the LAMP, breaking the SPELL and making Willis a rapist.

The Thinker

I magine what it must be LIKE to be him.   To KNOW that the POWER within is becoming STRONGER and STRONGER with EACH PASSING DAY.   To KNOW that he MUST RELAX and NOT LOSE it.   Otherwise it could mean COMPLETE DISASTER.

It's not like he ever WANTED it this way.   He'd always been someone who just FOUND himself THINKING these things.   Of course, EVERYONE thinks these things at ONE time or another.   Everyone has FANTASIES they CAN'T CONTROL, IDEAS they wish had NEVER OCCURRED to them.   It's all simply part of the plan. The HUMAN plan.

But THEN comes the SHAME.   And THEN THE GUILT!   And THEN...well it's too AWFUL to even CONSIDER, let alone describe.   So after MANY YEARS of having to COPE with it FULL-SCALE, there was ONLY ONE POSSIBLE SOLUTION!   And even THAT could be DEVASTATING.

NATURALLY, it didn't SEEM like such a great idea, but, when the ALTERNATIVE to his PROGRESS was CONSIDERED, it seemed the ONLY answer.   And in fact, MAYBE it wouldn't REALLY be so BAD at ALL.   Of course, it would most SURELY be WAY more DIFFICULT to pull off, than one would THINK.   Especially with the POWER being so STRONG!   But at LEAST, he was willing to go THROUGH with it, which was a WONDERFUL

SIGN. After all, COMPASSION was the KEY. Yet by THEN, he was FAR BEYOND CONTROLLING his compassion.   Even SUBCONSCIOUSLY. Because, there's ALWAYS a PART of him to OBJECT.   And THAT could be WAY DANGEROUS.   Like the PERSONALITY of his MIND as with EVERYONE ELSE'S is always in CONFLICT with itself.   And quite FRANKLY, WHOSE WOULDN'T be under THESE circumstances.

Now there are SOME who say, he didn't even HAVE the power.   They say he'd barked up the WRONG TREE.   Or they say that he was JUST CRAZY, that his MIND was playing TRICKS on him, perhaps as the result of an ACCIDENT he had when he was a KID, or some kind of ILLUSION which he was caused to have back then that he NEVER got OVER. But THAT'S a lot of CRAP, and HE KNEW it. And AFTER ALL, THOSE AFOREMENTIONED situations were just THE EXPERTS' THEORIES about him, like all OTHER explanations of what had been happening. Of course, if this were REALLY a case of someone just being CRAZY, they'd have ALREADY locked him UP and thrown away the fuckin' KEY!

Then there's the LESS COMMON theory that he'd ACTUALLY been GASLIGHTED.   That NOTHING BAD that ever happened to anyone was REAL, only a SET-UP to get BACK at him for something.   But WHO'D want to DO that to him, and WHY?   Much like the ILLUSION or young ACCIDENT theory, it DIDN'T MAKE SENSE!   He

HAD no known ENEMIES. He'd NEVER HAD a major ACCIDENT. And except for seeing a few MAGIC shows when he was a kid, he'd NEVER had any ILLUSIONS. Of course, he spent LOTS of time trying to REMEMBER, but trying to DO it as CAREFULLY as he COULD. NATURALLY. Because even trying to REMEMBER too HARD could be WAY DANGEROUS.

Every THOUGHT he had, every FEELING he FELT needed to be KEPT WRAPPED SO TIGHT, so it could be NIXED as QUICKLY as it COULD if it might HURT someone. And the AGONY of his ATTEMPTS at DOING so, could ONLY be topped by the DISASTERS he could bring OTHERS if he FAILED to DO so. For MANY OTHERS, this wouldn't be a problem. They'd just say, OH WELL, DON'T PISS me OFF, and you'll be FINE. And if even THEN someone ELSE had damaging thoughts, it would only be a PROBLEM for the VICTIMS, and the victims' LOVED ones.

But HE couldn't DEAL with it that way. After ALL, he HAD no known enemies, no adversaries, never even had a RIVAL. Sometimes he guessed it would be better if he HAD, because THEN at least MAYBE the POWER he had would be DRAINED OFF, somehow, and he'd NEVER have to WORRY about ANYTHING going wrong.

Obviously there was NOTHING anyone in either the MEDICAL or PSYCHIATRIC professions could do for him, as there was NO KNOWN CURE for what he had. So when he REALIZED he HAD the power, he began reading all KINDS of BOOKS and MANUALS about paranormal phenomena, as he KNEW how CAREFUL he had to BE in figuring out EXACTLY WHAT he had, WHAT he'd DONE because of what he HAD, and of COURSE, what he could DO about it WITH NO DEADLY SIDE EFFECTS!

And it had finally gotten to the POINT, where he had to just STOP and think as LOGICALLY and CAREFULLY as he COULD about it. To WEIGH and MEASURE EVERY SINGLE PRO and CON, as if the SAFETY of the ENTIRE WORLD DEPENDED on it. Because where HE was concerned, it REALLY did.

So he sat back, relaxed, thought of ALL the AWFUL THINGS that had happened HE had CAUSED. He thought about all the WARS and the DEVASTATING BLOODSHED THEY'D brought. He thought about all the SEEMINGLY NATURAL DISASTERS which had occurred, and the AMAZING DEATH toll THEY had taken. He thought about ALL the VIOLENCE that OCCURRED EACH and EVERY DAY between PEOPLE, ANIMALS and SPIRITS. And how the WORLD was NOTHING MORE than a WHIRLWIND of HATE and HORROR, and how the MORE he thought about it, the WORSE it GOT!

And the GUILT he felt for having CAUSED this UNSPEAKABLE PLETHORA of tragedy had MANI-FESTED itself WITHIN him, and by NOW had ACCUMULATED to the POINT where he SIMPLY WANTED to CEASE to EXIST, if for ONLY it could mean SOME repentance on his part.

So NOW he began to PRAY. And he PRAYED to WHOMEVER out there would LISTEN to him — whomever out THERE held CONTROL over his VERY FREE WILL of THOUGHT! And he simply BEGGED to NEVER AGAIN have a THOUGHT for as LONG as he should LIVE of ANY KIND of destruction whether it be MASSIVE or MINIMUM. And although he was UNABLE to FORGIVE himself for all the world-wide DAMAGE he had CAUSED throughout his LIFE, he WANTED and BEGGED to SOMEDAY be PURGED of ALL his SINS of ATROCITY in the AFTERLIFE. This MEANT HE wanted to SUFFER THERE at LEAST as much as he'd CAUSED all THOSE he'd caused to SUFFER. And he didn't WANT it to be SWIFT. He WANTED it to be LONG, PAINFUL and AGONIZING — PERHAPS even for the course of ETERNITY — for he TRULY BELIEVED NOW that NOBODY ALIVE deserved to SUFFER more than HE did.

Yet for NOW, his BIGGEST concern was in STOPPING any MORE of these AWFUL THINGS from HAPPENING as SOON as POSSIBLE. And while SUICIDE MIGHT be the answer, he COULDN'T be SURE — he HAD to KNOW in ABSOLUTION that his THOUGHT PROCESS was SO MINIMIZED, that there'd NO LONGER be ANY way he could affect ANYONE like that EVER AGAIN. And of course, if he were DEAD, he couldn't ACTUALLY KNOW for a FACT, that his

BRAIN WAVES would no LONGER cause more DESTRUCTION. However, if his THOUGHT PROCESS worked JUST ENOUGH for him to KNOW that he could NO LONGER think STRONGLY enough to CAUSE it, then he'd KNOW he'd SUCCEEDED. And his PRAYER for THIS was QUICKLY ANSWERED when he found an old ALL-PURPOSE DRILL in his BASEMENT, and FINALLY got up the NERVE to LOBOTOMIZE himself.

Of course, his POWER was IMAGINED. Like MY URGE to CREATE a CHARACTER who had to SUFFER like that. OVERWHELMING, isn't it?

A Very Strong Possibility

D eck the halls, fa, la, la, la, may the holidays bring JOY and GREAT FORTUNE for the coming YEAR, and ALL that HAPPY HISHPASH! Naturally, THERE'S the SPIRIT which can BRING a family TOGETHER and make their UNITY THAT MUCH STRONGER!

EVEN a family which had been BRUISED and BROKEN for so MANY fuckin' YEARS it was TRULY AMAZING ANY of them were still ALIVE! Of course, those that WERE were MUCH better off since their ORIGINAL FOUNDER and BREADWINNER was FINALLY serving 30 years to LIFE for the ATTEMPTED and VERY NEARLY SUCCESSFUL murder of his ex-wife. Which at this TIME of year had to be such a BLESSING, that a TREE, MISTLETOE and STOCKING stuffers should NOT even be NECESSARY.

However, THIS was a case where there were CHILDREN involved, and Meredith KNEW that it was TIME for THEIR comings DUE. Time for THEM to know the OTHER side of the COIN. Time for THEM to have the KIND of holiday SEASON they'd never had in their WILDEST fuckin' DREAMS! And the JOY it would SURELY BRING Mary and Joey could ONLY BEGIN to give Meredith back her SANITY.

After all, the HEALING process hadn't NEARLY begun yet. There was still MUCH to work THROUGH, which would SURELY take a few YEARS anyway. Meredith's SELF-RESPECT and SELF-ESTEEM LITERALLY HINGED on her NEW found CHILD-REARING skills, and THAT was THAT.

Finally getting to be the REAL MOTHER to Mary and Joey that she WAS would be HER gift from OLD SAINT NICK. After ALL, THEY'D both been NAMED after JESUS' parents, and there'd been a REASON for that. She and Hank had BEGUN their married life (or at LEAST HE had) with the INTENTION of bringing their offsprings UP in the HOLIEST MANNER POSSIBLE!

But looking back on it NOW, Meredith

BELIEVED it MAY have been the cause of their DEMISE. Maybe they went a LITTLE overboard. Because while Hank had been RAISED with the STRONGEST CHRISTIAN VALUES of ANYONE Meredith KNEW, it had ALSO become such an OBSESSION with HIS parents that it had ULTIMATELY rendered him a REBEL.

Since it was ONE thing to raise a family with strong values, it was QUITE ANOTHER THING ENTIRELY to INSIST that ONCE the CHILD had his OWN children he CONTINUE to EXTEND and FOLLOW that STRICT SYSTEM of VALUES and MORALITIES to the LETTER! And QUITE FRANKLY, Meredith couldn't figure out how Hank had GONE through his ENTIRE fuckin' CHILDHOOD WITH-OUT cracking up.

Which of COURSE was NO fuckin' excuse for him LOSING it in LATER life and TAKING it ALL OUT on THEM! Yet if there was ANY JUSTIFICATION at ALL for what HAPPENED, THAT may have BEEN IT, so NOW the REAL STRICT stuff had to GO to SPARE Mary and Joey.

The children now came running into the house after their snowball fight. And it didn't take long for Meredith to realize Joey was STILL pursuing Mary, though Mary was pretty upset about the goings-on.

"Get the fuck AWAY from me, you ASSHOLE!" she screamed, in a manner VERY SIMILAR to the way Meredith would often wail at Hank. Yet Joey caught hold of her and started to crack icicles all over her face and down her blouse.

"Take THAT, you SLIMY WHORE!" he bellowed, with the same type of intensity Hank would use with Meredith, only quite unaware he was copying a most HORRIFIC practice.

Mary screamed, bit and clawed at her brother's eyes, while Meredith did her best to separate them. "Hey, come ON, you 2. Santa Claus DOESN'T give PRESENTS to children who BEHAVE this way!"

"Ah, there AIN'T no fuckin' Santa Claus, you OLD BIMBO," stated Joey. At that point Meredith lost it all, and SLAPPED his face. He immediately let go of Mary and began to cry crocodile tears. Meredith was BESIDE herself. She couldn't BELIEVE what she'd done. This was NOT the answer. Because no matter how ANGRY and AGGRESSIVE these children were, THIS was the type of stuff which HAD to be UNLEARNED in the WORST fuckin' WAY. NO 2 WAYS! "Oh, Joey, I'm SO SORRY; PLEASE FORGIVE ME! I SWEAR it'll NEVER happen again," pleaded Meredith, as she rubbed his head and face in the spot she'd slapped him.

"Oh, RIGHT, like he didn't DESERVE it!" yelled Mary, as she shook the icicles out all over the floor. "Why don't you just take a BASEBALL bat to his fuckin' HEAD, the way DADDY did to YOU! And maybe THIS time he WON'T WAKE UP, even though YOU DID!"

Meredith KNEW the answer was NO VIO-

LENCE. The answer was DOING whatever it TOOK, and SAYING whatever she could SAY which would make these children SEE how much GREAT LOVE they'd been MISSING all these years. And Meredith also knew that in a way, it was actually FORTUNATE Joey was still CRYING a little, otherwise his RESPONSE to his sister's plea for Meredith to take his LIFE would most SURELY be MET with some form of PHYSICAL RETALIATION against her.

"I know," said Meredith finally, after trying to think of SOMETHING to say which would HOPEFULLY take the children's minds off of VIOLENCE, "what EXACTLY do you guys WANT for Christmas?"

"A CRASHER-BASHER TRAIN SET!" they both yelled together, as if Meredith had AMAZINGLY found the way to FINALLY bring PEACE and UNITY BETWEEN them. Although it SOUNDED like a pretty violent TOY, Meredith sensed their COMMON INTEREST in it was a GREAT SIGN they could FINALLY get along.

"All right, then," she said, "a Crasher-Basher train set it is!" It ABSOLUTELY worked like a CHARM for the moment. Joey now stopped crying, and for the REMAINDER of the DAY, Mary and Joey kept TALKING together about how much FUN they were EACH going to have with their new Crasher-Basher train set, and how they could HARDLY WAIT for it. But what impressed Meredith the MOST was how they seemed ANXIOUS to

SHARE the set, EVEN if it were ONLY since there'd be no POINT or FUN in the DEMOLITION of something UNLESS it REPRESENTED your RIVAL.

Unfortunately, the next day when Meredith went to the toy store to BUY it for them, she found they were all sold OUT of them. As was EVERY fuckin' store she TRIED. So after settling for a more CONSERVATIVE train set, only to find on Christmas morning Mary and Joey were so fuckin' P.O.-ED at her for NOT buying them the Crasher-Basher that they TRIED PUMMELING her with ALL their MIGHT, to the point where she CALLED the fuckin' COPS, she decided to check the WEB to find out if she could ORDER one. And she DID. But then she found Crasher-Basher train sets were being RECALLED for SAFETY. But she got them one ANYWAY, hoping it would KILL them. But being I'm NOT the cocksucker everyone SAYS, I'll write it just BURNED down their HOUSE and FINALLY made them BEHAVE.

The Thumber

MAN, that Leroy! WHAT a fuckin' EGGHEAD! When God was handing out BRAINS, He OVERDID it with him. I mean, it's ONE thing for a kid to be a better than average CHESS player, or a

SPELLING bee champ. But to have your fuckin' PHD by the age of 10, and then to teach SCIENCE at Harvard Medical Center one year later, and get to oversee all the grants and budgets of practically the ENTIRE fuckin' FINANCIAL COMMUNITY! Well, that was REAL GOOD for Leroy. He had a great head for FIGURES, COMPUTERS and PHYSICS. But looking back on it, there's one thing he fuckin' lacked, BIG time. STREET SMARTS! Yep. Leroy was a great inventor, a marvelous chemist, and a superb electronic specialist. But when it came to dealing with the HARSH REALITIES of LIFE, well, just let's just say he fuckin' BLEW it. Which in HINDSIGHT, really came as no fuckin' surprise to anyone that KNEW him. Leroy had a WAY of REALLY getting under the SKIN, sometimes. Because if you're some-one who was BLESSED with all those talents and skills which he WAS, the LAST fuckin' thing you want to do is rub it IN to the REST of the world. Of course, Leroy meant no HARM at all. In FACT, I KNOW for a fact that ALL his EFFORTS in life were DEFINITELY for the fuckin' BETTERMENT of humanity. And he DID accomplish MANY THINGS. Discovered CURES for BAD diseases, advanced the SPACE program FULL-SCALE, TAUGHT WELL.

You know what I THINK though? You know what I think Leroy could have USED at that POINT in his life where the LAST VESTIGES of his CHILD-HOOD were suddenly MELDING with the NEW PRESSURES of ADOLESCENCE, which of course in

Leroy's case were MULTIPLIED so fuckin' MUCH because of his GREAT INTELLIGENCE? I think he could have used some TOP QUALITY CUNT for himself. Fuck, I know I could have USED some at that point in MY life. Shit, I could use some RIGHT fuckin' NOW!

But enough about ME! This fuckin' story's about Leroy. About the man-boy who probably did too MUCH, WAY too fuckin' SOON. And in a WAY, this is ACTUALLY sort of a DEDICATION. Because Leroy was so EAGER and DETERMINED to SUCCEED, and IT'S SUCH a fuckin' SHAME what happened to him.

I REALLY IDOLIZED him in a way, you see. If he'd SOMEHOW been ABLE to acquire the STREET smarts which I pointed out a few fuckin' paragraphs ago, or even DEVOTED just a LITTLE of his life to SPECIAL WEAPONRY, he would have been a REALLY BOSS FIGUREHEAD.

And if I had the FORMULA he used to BUILD that AWESOME fuckin' TIME machine of his, I wouldn't be wasting all THIS fuckin' time, sitting around here, writing this crap. Well actually, I WOULD, but THEN, you see, I'd have a MUCH fuckin' HAPPIER place to start, now WOULDN'T I? Since THEN I'd have CHANGED HISTORY JUST for HIM!

It's pretty fuckin' IRONIC to NOTE here, that Leroy HIMSELF actually changed history. In a HUGE fuckin' WAY, even. In FACT, I KNOW for a FACT that HIS CHANGE in HISTORY was SO fuckin' MAJOR, that YOU'RE probably AFFECTED by it EVERY fuckin' DAY of your LIFE! Although you only THINK about it, if it ends up causing some kind of fuckin' VIOLENCE which involves you. Of course, you wouldn't KNOW that HISTORY had actually been CHANGED, unless you READ this fuckin' STORY.

Now needless to say, although if you're PRETTY fuckin' STUPID which you COULD very well BE, however if you're SMART enough to READ this, you probably already KNOW that Leroy was ANY-THING but VIOLENT. In FACT, he'd HOPED to be able to make this WORLD as PEACEFUL as the way the REST of the universe LOOKS from here. Except he wasn't going to kill everybody OFF to DO it. And THAT was a WONDERFUL DREAM, and quite FRANKLY, I'd try it MYSELF if I could figure out how to rebuild Leroy's TIME machine. I'd HAVE to, since the COCKSUCKERS that KILLED Leroy, ALSO busted it UP something fuckin' FIERCE!

And I think the BIGGEST mistake Leroy MADE concerning his time machine was letting ON about it to ANYONE. At least, ANYONE who used to fuckin' PICK on him all the time. But UN-FORTUNATELY, when he finished BUILDING it there was NOBODY AROUND but THEM for him to fuckin' GLOAT to. And NATURALLY, THEY, those SCUMFUCKERS being some of his BEST fuckin' STUDENTS at Harvard (wouldn't you fuckin' KNOW it) JEALOUS fuckin' DICKS, EVERY LAST TURDY fuckin' ONE of them, were out in the courtyard on the campus, when Leroy COMPLETED his great INVENTION and brought it OUT to SHOW them.

"Well, well, LOOK what little NERDY MADE for us," exclaimed one of the assholes to the others as they gargled on their beer.

"What is it, Leroy?" said one of the others. "Oh don't tell me, let me GUESS," quipped yet another. "It's a fuckin' PANSY holder for Professor Leroy to SIT in and JERK himself OFF!" Naturally, ALL the SCUMS laughed pretty fuckin' hard at this.

"No, it ISN'T; it's a time machine," said Leroy, in his typical NONCHALANT, THEY MAY BE DICKS, BUT THERE'S SOME GOOD IN EVERYONE kind of way.

"Oh, right, a TIME MACHINE, isn't THAT CUTE," said the final scum in the group, before spitting a mouthful of beer on Leroy.

"Perhaps you gentlemen would care to see a demonstration," said Leroy, his fuckin' dignity held intact by only God knows what. Before the others could react, Leroy had stepped into the time machine, flipped the power switch, and gone back exactly a hundred years to the second. "I believe they must be impressed now," he stated, while stepping out into 19th century Cambridge.

Everything looked pretty much the same—the night was clear, the courtyard green. Yet now the young men were wearing silk shirts, finely pressed trousers, close-cropped sideburns and stove pipe hats, while the young ladies wore long dresses to hide temptations and bonnets to compete with the stove pipes. And of course, the sounds of loud blaring motors and horns were replaced by neighs and clip-clops. And only MOMENTS after arriving, Leroy heard loud, male profanity coming from an adjacent alley.

"Fuck shoes! Fuck DEVICES which SLOW progress," came the angry shouts. Always one willing to help someone in need, Leroy ran over to find the young man had JUST FINISHED reshoeing his horse. He gave the man a quick thumbs-up. "WHY YOU IMPERTINENT LITTLE TWIT, HOW DARE YOU MAKE SUCH A GESTURE!"

"But I was simply congratulating you." Yet the man started to BEAT him, until he was rescued by some other students and ran back to his time machine before he got INJURED! When the others asked the beater what it was ABOUT, he told them about the THUMB gesture, and said it would have made more sense to CONGRATULATE him by showing the MIDDLE finger, instead of that UGLY THUMB. Of course, BOTH GESTURES SOON became SOLIDIFIED, and when Leroy RETURNED to the PRESENT he was BEATEN to DEATH by those SCUMS, who gave each other THUMBS-UPS before being sent away for life.

Shovelin' It

It had been an ABSOLUTELY BEAUTIFUL ceremony, and an EVEN NICER reception. The mood of LOVE had seemed to reach out and touch EVERYONE in ATTENDANCE. It was the REASON storybooks were WRITTEN, the FODDER of the MISTY-EYED, PERFECT WORLD worshipper.

Of course, everyone that KNEW Hank and Mabel knew they were the PERFECT COUPLE. She had LITERALLY been the girl next door for the past 17 years, and NOW they'd share the SAME house until the good Lord CALLED them home. And Hank had NO qualms after having been Mabel's BEST and OLDEST FRIEND, that this MARRIAGE would be working out. As neither did Mabel, who'd ALREADY spent many a day and night in the company of her FOREVER man, as CHILDREN with the same PLAYMATES and CLASSMATES, young ADULTS with common GOALS and DREAMS, and finally the STAGE was now SET for a LIFETIME of PURE WEDDED BLISS for both of them.

And even AS children together, sitting together on each other's PORCHES, reading FAIRY TALES of ROMANTIC HEROISM, there'd been MUCH TALK BETWEEN them about how GREAT it would be to share their OWN kind of heroic romance someday. Of course, in THEIR case, there'd be no HERO, no KNIGHT in shining ARMOR come to RESCUE his LOVING QUEEN from a DARK DUNGEON, or

HANDSOME PRINCE to call with a special glass
SLIPPER which turned out to belong to his LOVING
CINDERELLA, or a KISS to awaken a SLEEPING
PRINCESS after a 100 years of IMPRISONMENT. It
was the ULTIMATE FAIRY TALE come TRUE
WITHOUT ANY of the CONFLICT. How PERFECT
could it BE?

And EVEN during their ADOLESCENCE, there'd
ALWAYS been a STATE of COMPLETE and EX-
CLUSIVE MONOGAMY between them, as they were
RARELY SEEN NOT TOGETHER, when EITHER of
them was SEEN at ALL. So of COURSE, they were
QUITE the ENVY of all those couples who couldn't
REALLY HOLD it together, or even those SINGLE
people who spent most of THEIR free time in a
DAYDREAM FANTASY about when that 'SPECIAL
ONE' would come along.

Suffice it to SAY, they were VOTED a
UNANIMOUS 100% as the class couple in HIGH
SCHOOL, and together they found themselves a
very special COLLEGE where they EACH MAJORED
in HUMAN RELATIONS and did their BEST to help
OTHERS in relationships.

And by the time of their storybook WEDDING,
they'd made quite a NAME for themselves in
their own BUSINESS they'd started doing JUST
THAT, as HUNDREDS of couples a WEEK who
were STRUGGLING so AIMLESSLY to keep THEIR
relationships AFLOAT would CALL on them
REGULARLY with FANTASTIC RESULTS. So suffice

it to say, Hank and Mabel were all set both MATRIMONIALLY AND FINANCIALLY.

And what they TOLD ALL their clients who paid them TOP DOLLAR to help them to SECURE DESPERATE SITUATIONS was to JUST TRY to IMAGINE what life would be LIKE without the other PERSON in the picture. And while members of MANY of their couples would OFTEN SAY that this would be MOST WELCOME, Hank and Mabel would THEN suggest to them that they THEN try to IMAGINE all those HAPPY times between them they ONCE had (which of course, NONE of them could DENY they EVER HAD) being POSSIBLE without the OTHER one, and work together from THAT.

And when it FINALLY got to the POINT where BOTH PEOPLE in the couple were CRYING because they REALIZED that the OTHER person in their RELATIONSHIP HAD in FACT been RESPONSIBLE for those most HAPPY of times, then the MONEY for their BUSINESS had been QUITE WELL EARNED. And suffice it to SAY, Hank and Mabel's BUSINESS had been TOUTED QUITE HIGHLY in both many PSYCHIATRIC journals AND POPULAR MAG-AZINES and SYNDICATED NEWSPAPERS. And while there WERE SOME CYNICS who basically SAID that ANYONE can do VISUALIZATIONS without PAYING OTHERS to HELP them, UNLESS there was some kind of HYPNOSIS involved, then what was the POINT of BOTHERING with the type of BUSINESS that Hank and Mabel ran—like it was some kind of SHAM.

However, the RESULTS were MOST ASSUREDLY speaking VOLUMES in their FAVOR, and Hank and Mabel's PERSONALLY DEVELOPED TECHNIQUE of COUPLES VISUALIZATION could NOT REALLY be DUPLICATED WITHOUT them.   Unless you CALLED and ORDERED their INSTRUCTIONAL video.   WHICH, put them up OVER the MILLION DOLLAR mark.

SO NOW they were in their HONEYMOON suite, CELEBRATING the occasion of their most WONDERFUL marriage with CHAMPAGNE and fine MUSIC. They DANCED about their IN-CREDIBLY LUXURIOUS HOTEL room like CHILD-REN in the NIGHT discovering themselves locked in a CANDY store.

"Oh, my PRECIOUS, PRECIOUS ONE," exalted Mabel, as Hank dipped her before carefully placing a fresh, thorn-picked rose in her mouth. The sparkling light from the chandelier seemed to spin around them EXQUISITELY as they pirouetted about the floor.

"Oh, my MOST MARVELOUS LADY," Hank said right back. "If everyone could only KNOW how we've NOW become the world's KING and QUEEN, it would but SHOCK them so PROFUSELY."

Mabel gallantly removed the rose as she twirled about and handed it back to Hank so she could speak. "Oh, I think NOT, my BETROTHED," she continued, as she pivoted back. "For I KNOW only too WELL, that WE have SURELY become ROYALTY'S most HERALDED COUPLE by now."

Hank realized she was probably right. After ALL, EVERYTHING they'd always DONE they'd done so BEAUTIFULLY TOGETHER. And LOOK where it had GOTTEN them. It seemed like ALL between them had ALWAYS been JUST SO BLESSED, and NOTHING could EVER CHANGE that.

"You know what it seems like to ME," said Hank, as they kept dancing like they could go ON DOING it forever.

"What, my darling, my radiant love, my EVERLASTING ALL!"

"It seems that ALL between us has ALWAYS been JUST SO BLESSED, and NOTHING could EVER CHANGE that."

"You've SURE SAID a MOUTHFUL, my SWEET. Perhaps a little more CHAMPAGNE, and MY ways of expressing MYSELF would be EQUALLY as PROFOUND!" If she wanted more champagne, then more she'd HAVE. After ALL, MUTUAL UNDER-STANDING was what it was all ABOUT.

"All right, my love. Let's REST for a MOMENT and pour us some MORE. But don't you think for a SECOND that you'd need to be under the influence of CHAMPAGNE, in order to EXPRESS yourself in a PROFOUND MANNER. You, Mrs. Mabel Tatlebaum are as PROFOUND a person as I KNOW! And that ALSO includes MANY who are DECEASED!"

"MY, how you DO carry on, my love," she responded. "AND you ALSO know how to get a HONEYMOON off to a ROARING start. Not that ANY of this SURPRISES me in the LEAST. After ALL, like we ALWAYS tell our CLIENTS, if EACH MEMBER of the couple goes all OUT to make the OTHER one HAPPY, then the MATCH is made in HEAVEN."

"I'll drink to that, my dear," said Hank, after pouring.

Of course, the HAPPIEST moment AFTER their WEDDING would be when Mabel did Hank's BEST MAN, and Hank did the MAID OF HONOR.

The Bear Truth

A utumn was fresh in the air with all the restless energy of everyone on the SCHOOL grounds taking center stage. It was as if the DISAPPOINTMENT of being BACK at school for another 9 months hadn't kicked in yet in ANYONE THERE— STUDENTS and FACULTY ALIKE. But of course, THIS was the type of region where AUTUMN could QUELL ANY kind of disappointment, save for a WAY TOO EARLY WINTER. But when CONSIDERING what the residents of THIS small town were ACCUSTOMED too, even THAT sort of thing could be COPED with in a VERY POSITIVE WAY.

The students were receiving their new but used TEXTBOOKS and ALREADY some were SCRIBBLING NONSENSE and PROFANITY into them. It was part of this SMALL TOWN'S TRADITION, to leave your MARK on what would be passed DOWN to future generations to remind THEM of how SOME things would NEVER change.

Of course, in every CLASSROOM there was a STUDENT who felt that THIS TYPE of tradition did NOT CONTRIBUTE to the BETTERMENT of ANY-ONE, but SIMPLY SHOWED future generations the JUVENILITY of his OWN. Not to MENTION getting HIMSELF in a BIG HEAP of TROUBLE if he got CAUGHT. And in THIS class, it was Raymond McGann.

He'd ALWAYS sort of been the TEACHER'S PET, the PERENNIAL KISS-UP if you will. Of course, the FUTURE DID INDEED look BRIGHT for this young man, as he ALWAYS kept his nose to the GRINDSTONE.

UNFORTUNATELY, and UNBEKNOWNST to Raymond, but VERY SOON to be DISCOVERED by him, his NEW TEACHER, Mr. Willoughby had a TRACK record like NO OTHER TEACHER Raymond had EVER KNOWN here. He was the STRICTEST TYPE of DISCIPLINARIAN, who BELIEVED QUITE STRONGLY in CORPORAL PUNISHMENT, and as far as Mr. Willoughby was CONCERNED, EVERY student was SOME kind of OFFENDER, and

NOTHING ACCOMPLISHED or GOOD a student EVER DID, could NOT have some kind of ULTERIOR MOTIVE BEHIND it.

So when the student BEHIND Raymond CONSTRUCTED, then SAILED a paper AIRPLANE toward Mr. Willoughby, it was Raymond who found himself WRITING on the BLACKBOARD at the BACK of the CLASSROOM a thousand times, the PHRASE, I SHOULDN'T MISBEHAVE IN CLASS, and THEN HAVING to do 3 TIMES as much HOME-WORK as the OTHER STUDENTS, and ALL THIS after HAVING to STAY after SCHOOL for 2 HOURS that VERY FIRST DAY, CLAPPING out BLACK-BOARD ERASERS and SCRUBBING the FLOOR and WALLS of the CLASSROOM. So suffice it to say, Raymond had begun the SCHOOL year with the WORST and MOST UNIMAGINABLE day of his life. And through it all he had OTHER ISSUES which needed to be worked out. And it didn't LOOK like Mr. Willoughby was going to be at ALL either SYMPATHETIC or UNDERSTANDING.

Even the STUDENT who ACTUALLY THREW the paper AIRPLANE felt BAD about what had HAPPENED to Raymond as a result of what HE'D DONE. Of course, he ALSO felt it would have been a LOT WORSE if HE'D been the ONE who'd been PUNISHED.

However, the UP side of the situation was that neither HE, nor any of the OTHER MOST MISCHIEVOUS STUDENTS would be ACTING UP for a LONG TIME. At LEAST until they were ABLE to figure out a FOOLPROOF WAY to make sure that only the most WELL-BEHAVED students like Raymond would ALWAYS have to take the RAP for THEIR MONKEYSHINES. Yup. Human nature in the CLASSROOM. You just had to LOVE it.

As far as Raymond was concerned, the extra HOMEWORK he'd had to do was a BLESSING. Raymond was an EXTREMELY STUDIOUS BOY who ACTUALLY LOVED WRITING things, and FIGURING THINGS OUT. And at LEAST Mr. Willoughby had NOT decided to contact Raymond's PARENTS about the events which had taken place in the classroom. Or the EVENT in PARTICULAR with the paper AIRPLANE he was OBVIOUSLY QUITE CERTAIN Raymond had been RESPONSIBLE for. Because if he HAD done that, the AFTERMATH would have been NOT NEARLY as pleasant.

UNFORTUNATELY, Raymond STILL FELT that in SPITE of his getting off on QUITE the wrong FOOT with Mr. Willoughby on the first DAY, he was CONFIDENT he could CHANGE that. He was WRONG.

So when Raymond showed UP the next MORN-ING for class with NO HOMEWORK assignment on his person, it made for a MOST DIFFICULT INTERACTION for him. ESPECIALLY since he was SUPPOSED to have 3 TIMES as MUCH as ANY OTHER STUDENT in the CLASS.

"Well, Mr. —," demanded Mr. Willoughby, solemnly. "About your HOMEWORK. What EXACTLY do you have to SAY for yourself? And before you SPEAK, you'd best think about what you're going to say MIGHTY CAREFULLY. Because THAT will make the DIFFERENCE in the SEVERITY of your PUNISHMENT. Have I MADE MYSELF QUITE CLEAR to you, Mr. McGann?"

Raymond nodded slowly, THOROUGHLY DREADING whatever LAY AHEAD for him. Of course, he HATED to LIE, especially when it would SURELY come to back to HAUNT him BIG time. But NOW even the TRUTH didn't seem too PROMISING. So after spending the next 5 seconds weighing the PROS and CONS of what his ANSWER would be, like his LIFE depended on it, Raymond said the ONLY thing he could THINK of. "A BEAR ate my homework."

The students' laughter was IMMEDIATELY stifled by the HORRIFIC and THUNDEROUS bellow of "SILENCE!" by Mr. Willoughby, who then PROMPTLY picked Raymond UP by the COLLAR of his shirt and HELD him in mid-air for about 30 seconds. Frightened out of his mind, Raymond began to cry before Mr. Willoughby finally put him down.

This time Raymond would have to write the phrase, I'LL NEVER LIE ABOUT AND ALWAYS DO MY HOMEWORK on the blackboard at the back of the room 2000 times, stay after school AGAIN to clap out erasers and scrub the walls and floor of the classroom, and THIS time have 6 times as much homework to do for the NEXT day. In addition to all THAT, THIS time Mr. Willoughby sent a NOTE HOME with Raymond telling his PARENTS ALL about his BEHAVIOR, which THEY had to SIGN and send BACK with HIM. So suffice it to SAY, the SECOND day of school had QUICKLY become the NEW WORST DAY of Raymond McGann's LIFE. At LEAST YESTERDAY when he'd stayed after school, his parents figured he'd been VOLUNTEERING for something SCHOLASTIC AT school, and didn't QUESTION him about what TOOK him so LONG to get HOME. But that was OBVIOUSLY NOT going to work TODAY with the NOTE he had. Of course, DEEP in the back of Raymond's MIND, the SHOCK-ING NOTION of TRYING to FORGE his parents' SIGNATURES was rearing its UGLY HEAD. But Raymond KNEW he'd never get AWAY with it, any MORE than he HADN'T gotten away with NOT TURNING in his HOMEWORK.

However, Raymond's PARENTS NEVER GOT the note. In FACT, after Raymond left SCHOOL, he was NEVER SEEN AGAIN. As was INDICATED EARLIER, he had some ISSUES. The BIGGEST ONE was the hungry bear who ATE him, after the NOTE hadn't been ENOUGH to fill him UP.

Diggin' It

I AM and always HAVE been a DRIFTER of sorts. I MOVE from town to town, leaving my mark on every community in which I STOP with a most HEART FELT remembrance. Yet NOBODY really knows who I am. Folks just kind of SEE me as and when I'm NEEDED, like the HEAD of the CLEAN-up crew at their local PARKS who keeps it as CLEAN as a WHISTLE. Yet I've been around LONG enough to figure that my FACE and HUSTLE always PRECEDE all ELSE about my REPUTATION. I WOULDN'T HAVE it any OTHER WAY!

Because I'm DEFINITELY someone who BE-LIEVES in the VALUE of KEEPING BUSY—of ESTABLISHING myself as ONE who's ALWAYS WILLING to make himself USEFUL. And THIS kind of LIFESTYLE has DONE QUITE WELL by ME for MANY YEARS now. However, I'm NOT one who tends to GLOAT or BRAG about myself—I more or less just STATE my TRUE PHILOSOPHIES of LIFE, whenever I FEEL there's a POINT to be made.

Like I haven't ALWAYS felt on TOP of things like I do now. But NOW I TRULY THINK there was a REASON for that. Like in LIFE, I feel there are MANY TWISTS and TURNS and PEAKS and VALLEYS. And it has to DO with SIMPLY FINDING oneself. Which it OFTEN TAKES SO much LONGER than one EXPECTS or HOPES. But THIS is what MAKES it SO WORTHWHILE when it DOES happen.

And this applies to EVERYONE, NOT JUST MYSELF. So PLEASE KEEP that in MIND, the next time you FEEL WHATEVER you're DOING isn't PANNING OUT the WAY you'd hoped.

Like there WAS a time in my life, when I TRULY FELT that WHATEVER I'd ACCOMPLISHED had been MINIMIZED SO to the POINT where I ACTUALLY got it in my HEAD, that I'd never get ANYWHERE. All my KNOWLEDGE of the basic ELEMENTS of CHEMISTRY which ever since being so SMALL I just HAD to HAVE, like I KNEW it HAD to be my CALLING, wasn't HELPING me to get ANYWHERE. Of course, as a CHILD, the dream was of SOMEDAY becoming a MAD SCIENTIST, and INVENTING CHEMICALS that could do EVERY-THING from MAKING PEOPLE'S PERSONALITIES change DRASTICALLY, to TURNING them into DIFFERENT THINGS and ANIMALS, to ENABLING them to FLY, to GIVING them OTHER AMAZING POWERS, like to DISAPPEAR into THIN AIR, ONLY TO REAPPEAR somewhere ELSE, or MAKE them-selves INVISIBLE, or PASS through MATTER, etc. My FANTASIES sort of RAN the GAMUT, as they say.

Of course, the CLOSEST I ever came to ANY of that stuff was in my TEENAGE years, when I began EXPERIMENTING with all kinds of MIND altering CHEMICALS. And suffice it to SAY, at THAT point I'd begun to have enough KINDS of hallucinations to make all that AFOREMENTIONED stuff seem

QUITE REAL.

Yet when I FINALLY GREW OUT of my DRUG stage of LIFE, a LOT of which had to DO with me nearly DYING from OVERDOSING on them one STORMY NIGHT, I REALIZED NOW the ONLY way I was EVER going to ACHIEVE those DREAMS of chemical SUPREMACY was with an EDUCATION.

And SO, I began to WORK my way through COLLEGE. And I was a REALLY GOOD STUDENT. However, it was at THIS point in my life when I REALIZED that those CHILDHOOD FANTASIES of SUCH BIZARRE CHEMICAL USE were SOME-WHAT BEYOND my ABILITY. Try as I MIGHT to MIX and BREW and STIR and SHAKE, I could NEVER FIND I'd INVENTED ANYTHING too WEIRD. And of course, the SUGGESTIONS I received from my PROFESSORS to maybe SOMEDAY work in either the MEDICAL or PHARMACEUTICAL profession didn't really bode WELL with me. Even though I was an ADULT now, with a BETTER than AVERAGE MIND for CHEMICAL CREATION, I STILL HELD FAST to my DREAM of becoming a MAD SCIENTIST, WHATEVER the HELL that meant.

Which I realize NOW was SIMPLY another SIGN for me to SUCCEED at something ELSE. So what I DID one day was to just SIT BACK and CON-TEMPLATE the TRUE MEANING of the TERM, "MAD SCIENTIST." And then I CAME to a pretty FASCINATING CONCLUSION. Which was SIMPLY that a MAD SCIENTIST was a PERSON who through the USE of some KIND of SCIENCE, was able to HOLD some TYPE of STRANGE POWER over OTHERS. Then when I thought MORE about it, I DECIDED to NIX the STRANGE part. Because when you GOT RIGHT DOWN to it, POWER was POWER. And BEING that I was GETTING EVER OLDER but not RICHER, I DECIDED one day to INCORPORATE the CONCEPT of having POWER over PEOPLE with the ACT of making MONEY. And it would ALL BE THROUGH SCIENCE!

Suffice it to say, it's become a real life DREAM come TRUE. And the AMAZING thing was, I'd ALREADY been INVOLVED in what would EVEN-TUALLY AMOUNT to this DREAM COME TRUE, ONCE I was ABLE to SUPPLEMENT it with SCIENCE.

In OTHER words, I was STILL the LABORER I'd BEEN to pay for my COLLEGE tuition and OTHER expenses. And while the CALLUSES I GOT all over my HANDS at FIRST, and the OFTEN OCCURRING SORENESS in my JOINTS had MADE the job QUITE UNPLEASANT THEN, I'd NOW begun to REALIZE there was QUITE a PROFIT to be made doing this ACTIVITY. Because it was SOMETHING that UN-LIKE a LOT of OTHER JOB RELATED ACTIVITIES would ALWAYS have a DEMAND. And while there could ALWAYS be the chance of a STRIKE from the UNION I was IN, there was NO ACTUAL MONOPOLY on the POSITION, and I'D SURELY be

FREE to work for MYSELF, FREE and CLEAR, if I DIDN'T LIKE the UNION CONDITIONS. And what's MORE, there'd ALWAYS BE MORE of that kind of work AVAILABLE no matter WHERE I ENDED UP GOING! As WELL as the POTENTIAL to make some REAL GOOD MONEY, EVEN if the UNION to which I'd BELONGED had SUDDENLY DECIDED to DISCHARGE ME for REASONS of INSUBORDINATION!

FORTUNATELY, it NEVER ACTUALLY came DOWN to that. I QUICKLY REALIZED that the POTENTIAL was there for ME to make TONS of CASH by SECRETLY ADDING to my PROFESSION a TWIST of my OWN SCIENCE!

Of course, when you get right DOWN to it, my JOB WAS science. It was the SIMPLE ACT of LEVERAGE against GRAVITY MULTIPLIED by the QUANTITY of NECESSITY.

But what I was FINALLY ABLE to DO one day, after giving it MUCH REFLECTION was ADD to it my VERY FAVORITE BRAND of SCIENCE, which of course was CHEMISTRY. And suffice it to SAY, I FINALLY was ABLE to MIX a FORMULA together, which while it was not so TOTALLY UNUSUAL enough to FREAK out the WORLD, it DID have an EXTREMELY SHOCKING effect on THOSE to whom I was ABLE to APPLY it. And up to that POINT, the ONLY OTHER type of CHEMISTRY USED in MY particular trade involved the EMBALMING process. Of course, THIS END of it really had NOTHING to

DO with ME.

What I had MOST to gain by the PRODUCTION of this CHEMICAL FORMULA of mine was PROFIT, TRAVEL and the MEANS and REASONS to continue ACHIEVING BOTH. You see, the BOTTOM LINE HERE was SIMPLY PRODUCTION = SUPPLY and DEMAND, and what I JUST had to make ABSOLUTELY SURE of was that NOBODY WOULD EVER find OUT that MY PRODUCTION was MOSTLY RESPONSIBLE for all that SUPPLY and DEMAND, which of COURSE is WHY I must NEVER STAY in ONE PLACE VERY LONG after I've POISONED the WHOLE WATER supply with my SPECIAL FORMULA. Yet to THIS DAY, I'm PROBABLY the BEST PAID GRAVE DIGGER in the WORLD, and as for CALLUSES and SORES, HEY, NO PROBLEM!

Boraxo Blues

G osh, DARN, if baby Chuckie wasn't cute as the DICKENS. He had that sweet, innocent dimply look which said to the world, "I'll bet you're just DYING to take me home, and cuddle and play with me for the REST of ETERNITY." Of course, to those who could read between the lines, the message was more like, "proceed with COMPLETE CAUTION,

OTHERWISE, I'LL DRIVE you totally NUTZO!"

And one of those people who could read RIGHT between the lines with baby Chuckie was his mother, Maude. After all, the TRUE MATERNAL INSTINCT was the most REVEALING of them ALL.

Maude knew that baby Chuckie simply LIVED for the AFFECTION of all those POOR SAPS he could DRAW IN to his world. And then wait for JUST the RIGHT MOMENT to come a POUNCIN'. Like at the DAY care center, with the teacher, who NEVER SUSPECTED baby Chuckie could have POSSIBLY been responsible for putting EVERY SINGLE PIECE from ALL the kiddie board games they HAD down her blouse. Or the GOOD HUMOR man, who was NOW afraid to even drive his TRUCK through baby Chuckie's NEIGHBORHOOD, out of concern that as he was driving off with all his PROFITS, he'd SUDDENLY find his TRUCK and HIMSELF bombarded by EVERY FLAVOR of Italian ICE he sold. APPARENTLY, Italian Ice was baby Chuckie's FAVORITE. But OBVIOUSLY not JUST for EATING. Of course, the CLERK at 7/11 knew how baby Chuckie could be even MORE vicious with SLURPIES!

But let's FACE it, you STILL had to LOVE the kid. So WHAT if he gave his GRANDMA an ULCER by pretending to be CHOKING on a CHICKEN WING, after she'd gone to SO MUCH TROUBLE to FILLET it for him. Or CAUSE Aunt Mary to FALL by tying her SHOELACES together. Or DRAW a

GOATEE on Dear Abby, whom his mother read every DAY, which IRONICALLY prompted her to WRITE to Dear Abby for ADVICE on what to DO about baby Chuckie's ANTICS.

"Dear, Stumped In Sacramento. I've ALWAYS WANTED to SEE what I LOOKED like with FACIAL HAIR. In FACT, I've ACTUALLY had a HIDDEN DESIRE to have a SEX CHANGE, which YOUR REVELATION of this CUTE SILLINESS from YOUR BABY SON has MADE me DECIDE to come CLEAN about. As for what to DO about his BEHAVIOR, well, S.I.S., if I were YOU I wouldn't WORRY too MUCH about it. I mean it's NOT like he's causing you DEPRESSION or starting a NUCLEAR WAR! In fact, he sounds as CUTE as a BUTTON, and I'd LOVE to MEET him MYSELF. As for my ADVICE to YOU, S.I.S., it can be summed up in 3 little words, LIGHTEN UP, LADY! Very truly yours, Abby. P.S. — If you HAVEN'T TRASHED your baby's special TOUCH-up of my PICTURE, I'd LOVE for you to SEND it to me. In fact, I'd be MORE than happy to SPRING for the POSTAGE."

"I don't BELIEVE this," thought Maude, as she shook her head. "He's even got Dear Abby snowed. Well, then MAYBE she's right."

And so Maude sat back, sipped her coffee, and let her mind WANDER a little. It was a pretty nice day, and after doing her morning chores around the HOUSE, she'd take baby Chuckie with her when she went grocery shopping, and if he was REALLY

GOOD, she'd take him for a NICE WALK in the PARK.

"Oh, who'm I trying to KID. He'll do SOME-THING to wreck havoc. If he doesn't SPIT up all over someone in the CHECK-out line, he'll BREAK WIND, or try to SWIPE a piece of CANDY. Face it, Maude, the kid's a TOTALLY MANIPULATIVE little BEAST. Aw, but what the HELL, he's MY totally MANIPULATIVE LITTLE BEAST. And I'm STUCK with him, come HELL or high WATER. And I wouldn't HAVE it any OTHER WAY, RIGHT? Look, Maude, if YOU ACTUALLY SURVIVE MOTHER-HOOD with this little guy, YOU'LL have EARNED yourself a NOBEL PEACE PRIZE! Oh, my God, Maude, will you LOOK what you've LET HAPPEN to yourself. You've been REDUCED to the POINT where you can't HELP having these THINKING CONVERSATIONS. And it's your OWN FAULT. And if you DON'T STOP DOING it, it'll MAKE YOU CRAZY before you're 40!"

Suddenly the phone rang.

"AAAH! Oh, come ON, Maude, GET a GRIP, WILL YOU? Hello. Oh, HI, honey. You know you STARTLED me. Yeah, I was RIGHT in the MIDDLE of one of those special MIND conversations I have with myself over YOUR SON. Yeah, I KNOW I'll make myself CRAZY that WAY. That was the topic of CONVERSATION."

And so Maude spoke for a little while to her loving husband, Jeff, the BREADWINNER of the family, and of course, the loving FATHER of baby Chuckie. And of course, she had a HARD TIME not ENVYING him his position, in a SAFE place, UNREACHABLE from baby Chuckie in his nice cozy occupation down at the sewerage plant.

But after that it was BUSINESS as usual for both Maude, Jeff AND baby Chuckie. It was time for ALL of them to RESUME their daily routines. And somehow they ALL REALIZED that EVEN THOUGH they may be in different LOCATIONS from time to time, throughout the day, that EVERYTHING EACH one DID was somewhat INTERDEPENDENT with EVERYTHING the OTHER ones did.

And with THAT in mind, Maude went about the PROCEDURE of doing the family's LAUNDRY. Since JEFF'S CLOTHES were always the SMELLIEST, she'd always give them the FULL treatment—Boraxo HAD to be mixed in. Of course, in MOST families just starting out, the BABY'S clothes were usually the SMELLIEST, but since Jeff worked with EXCREMENT all day long—even more than baby Chuckie was capable of producing in an ENTIRE WEEK—THIS was ACTUALLY the EXCEPTION which PROVED the RULE. But of course, Maude was more than okay with this situation; after all, she'd MARRIED Jeff for BETTER or WORSE, and between HIS JOB and THEIR BABY, she could REALLY HOLD her OWN. And when you got right DOWN to it, that was what it was ALL ABOUT.

After she BEGAN the intense chore of doing the

laundry, Maude decided to run the BATH water, for a little while so it would be ALL READY for baby Chuckie, right after the laundry was DONE. She'd basically gotten the TIMING down JUST RIGHT—knowing EXACTLY how long the clothes would take to DRY, so she could be changed into them HERSELF and READY to give baby Chuckie his BATH right AFTERWARDS. And of course, TODAY would be like every OTHER wash day. Or so she THOUGHT.

After drawing the bath to MAXIMUM TEM-PERATURE, she TOOK the box of Mr. Bubble and poured its contents into the tub. That way it would be ready JUST in time, after Maude had CHANGED into her CLEAN, DRY CLOTHES. The water would have cooled off JUST the way baby Chuckie ALWAYS LOVED it, and be FILLED with BUBBLES GALORE. In spite of everything, Maude felt she had this MOTHER and WIFE stuff down pretty well.

For a moment, she actually FORGOT who she was DEALING with, and didn't even NOTICE BUBBLES on her CLOTHES in the PASSIVITY of the MOMENT. However, after putting baby Chuckie in the TUB, who GIGGLED profusely, though HE had NO BUBBLES, she realized why Jeff's clothes still smelled of the sewer, and why she HAD BUBBLES. The little guy had switched Mr. Bubble with Boraxo!

Simplex Stereotyping

P arks the butler was waiting downstairs. He'd been asked to see the new suit Mr. Regais had just purchased at Sax 5th Avenue.

Of course, Mr. Regais respected his opinion, BIG time. After all, Parks had once been very involved in the garment industry. His family had owned a textile mill just a few years earlier. Yet due to the VAST MODERNIZATION of the industry, his family had eventually been forced to declare BANK-RUPTCY.

Naturally, there was still much which came in quite handy in the knowledge and experience which went with such a history. Among them was knowledge of all kinds of fabrics and cloth, and the trend for the type of demand and value which they held.

"MY, sir, but if you don't mind my saying so, you look UTTERLY FABULOUS," stated Parks, as Mr. Regais came downstairs and into the drawing room. "I'm sure if Parks and Sons could have found a way to mass produce material like THAT, we'd still be in business and I wouldn't be..." He broke off, realizing he hadn't MEANT it like that.

"It's okay, Parks, I understand. I know what you were about to say. You could be a senior partner at Parks and Sons and you wouldn't have to be working as a butler for me." Mr. Regais reached into his pocket and handed Parks a fairly large bill.

"No, REALLY, sir, that WON'T be necessary. I'm ALL RIGHT."

"Okay," said Mr. Regais, putting the bill back in his pocket. "I just didn't want you to FORGET how APPRECIATED you REALLY ARE around here, THAT'S all."

"Of COURSE, sir," said Parks, feeling like a COMPLETE FOOL for not taking the bill. He'd seen it was a 50, and he HIMSELF was saving up to buy a nicer suit than any one he already owned. NOW he'd have to wait THAT MUCH LONGER. And if NOTHING ELSE, he'd learned his lesson about when to keep his mouth shut.

"The suit DOES look pretty spiffy, if I DO say so, DOESN'T it, Parks?" Mr. Regais was inspecting it in the mirror on the wall. "And of COURSE, in a way I have YOUR PEOPLE to THANK for it. Then again, I suppose I have MY people to thank for it TOO, when you get right DOWN to it. After all, WE'RE the ones who got to PICK all that WONDER-FUL COTTON for YOUR people, after YOUR people were KIND enough to HAUL us AGAINST OUR WILL all the WAY from Africa for that VERY PURPOSE. IRONIC, ISN'T it, Parks?"

This routine of Mr. Regais had now gotten QUITE OLD, and for Parks, it was one of the FEW DOWN SIDES of working for him. After all, the NEXT thing he'd do was point out how Parks' PEOPLE had once owned a WHOLE PLANTATION of SLAVES, while HIS people had an ENTIRE RACE

WORKING that plantation. As much as Parks HATED the CONCEPT of slavery, it was TIMES LIKE THIS when he ONLY WISHED that it hadn't been an ELEGANT FRENCH family, according to the HISTORY of Mr. Regais, who'd traced his family TREE back many TIMES, only to discover it was THIS FAMILY who'd DECIDED to set his family FREE as SLAVES but STILL keep them ON as WELL-PAID SERVANTS. Because it was OBVIOUS that in SPITE of their GREAT GENEROSITY to Mr. Regais' ANCESTORS, much of their NATURAL RUDENESS had been DIRECTLY INHERITED BY Mr. Regais. Of course, if OTHER things had happened differently then Parks would SURELY be running his FAMILY'S FORMER COMPANY, instead of WORKING as the FOOT licker to THIS guy. Of course, when he THOUGHT about it, Parks COULD see the cloud's SILVER LINING. As after all, like his father had TOLD him so MANY times, "Son, no matter HOW bad you may THINK you have it, REMEMBER you'll ALWAYS have the family NAME to fall back on." Parks couldn't help but CHUCKLE at THIS memory.

"Something FUNNY, Parks?" asked Mr. Regais, in his typical if it's something that CONCERNS YOU it must be MY BUSINESS TOO sort of way. "Because if it's something that CONCERNS YOU it must be MY BUSINESS TOO."

"No, sir. I simply felt a SLIGHT CHILL coming on, THAT'S all." Mr. Regais looked around like he couldn't figure out WHY.

"Well, Parks, since you're my FAVORITE BUTLER, you're MORE than WELCOME to feel FREE to turn up the HEAT. I'll COMPROMISE."

"Well, sir, that's REALLY VERY TOUCHING, when you consider that I'm your ONLY butler, and the more HEAT you use, the less MONEY you'll have to give ME a PAY RAISE any time soon."

Mr. Regais now looked as FLABBERGASTED as Parks felt. "Is something TROUBLING you, Parks? Because the LAST thing I NEED is a DISGRUNTLED EMPLOYEE, which, in case you need REMINDING, was the VERY PHILOSOPHY that ENABLED me to ELEVATE myself to this MOST ENVIABLE FINANCIAL POSITION!"

"Yes, Mr. Regais, I'm ONLY TOO AWARE of how YOU KNOW how to TREAT people. How could I NOT be, since you OBVIOUSLY LOVE to keep REMINDING me at EVERY OPPORTUNITY! Would it NOT be ENOUGH if I were to PROMPTLY DROP DOWN on my HANDS and KNEES, and PROFUSELY PROCEED to BEG your FORGIVENESS for your ANCESTORS' SLAVERY? I mean, with ALL DUE RESPECT, sir, did you EVER STOP to think where you'd be TODAY, if it WEREN'T for slavery?"

"PARKS! That will be QUITE ENOUGH. If YOU have a particular ISSUE on your mind at this moment, then I'll be MORE than HAPPY to HEAR it in FULL. However, you're NOT making OUR relationship any EASIER by SNIPPING at my

PSYCHE like this. Now I feel I'm a REASONABLE MAN. And in all the YEARS you've been WITH me, I've taken the BEST CARE of you. Yet you OFTEN SEEM RESENTFUL of me of late. And in order for our SITUATION to WORK, I NEED to KNOW WHY! Because I simply CANNOT nor WILL NOT keep someone ON with me, who SEEMS to be CARRYING a HUGE CHIP on his shoulder. It's simply NOT the way I OPERATE!" Parks tried to think carefully before he said what he HOPED would appease Mr. Regais and NOT cost him his job.

"All right, sir. I'll just say what I FEEL and be DONE with it. I FEEL that YOU, Mr. Regais tend to DWELL, and I use the term 'DWELL,' LOOSELY, but I REALLY THINK you tend to DWELL on the NORMS of our SITUATION being RADICALLY REVERSED. You seem to SEE me as the white BASTARD, who thinks he DESERVES to be where YOU are. And YOU'RE the FORMERLY POOR and OPPRESSED NEGRO who's FINALLY managed to TURN the tables on ME. And sir, quite FRANKLY, it SEEMS like ALL you've DONE for the past 6 MONTHS or so, is to RUB it in my FACE! And with ALL DUE RESPECT, sir, QUITE FRANKLY, I RESENT your ATTITUDE. Because while my ANCESTORS may have had it QUITE BETTER than YOURS did, MY ancestors are WAY DIFFERENT from ME. And in CASE you hadn't NOTICED, Mr. Regais, if you TOOK and COMPARED OUR lives, SIDE by SIDE, and BIT by BIT, I'd SAY there'd be LITTLE or NO

RESEMBLANCE between OURSELVES and our ANCESTORS." Parks was THANKFUL that Mr. Regais was now SMILING.

"I'm SORRY, Parks. I'll try to be more UNDER-STANDING. But right NOW I'm HUNGRY for BREAKFAST. How about some Aunt Jemima?"

"Yes, sir." Of course, some things would NEVER change.

Who the Fuck SENT You, ANYWAY?

You people are UNBELIEVABLE! Don't know a GREAT THING when it COMES YOUR WAY! Wouldn't know a GIFTHORSE if it JUMPED UP and BIT you in the fuckin' OVARIES! Or WHEREVER.

Well I'm JUST going to let you KNOW, I'm NOT ABANDONING this PROJECT no matter WHAT you do. You can TAUNT me, PUNCH me, KICK me, SPIT on me, ANYTHING at ALL. I'm going to STICK WITH it to the VERY END! And IN the VERY END, I MAY be the WORSE for WEAR. And YOU'LL STILL HATE my fuckin' GUTS! And you WON'T EVEN KNOW what I've DONE for you! Well, you may KNOW, but by THAT time, you'll FEEL so BAD about the way you've TREATED me DEEP DOWN, but because of ALL your fuckin' PRIDE, you'll

NEVER ADMIT IT!

Now SEE, THAT'S ONE of the REASONS I'm HERE. Of course, it's ONLY one of MANY. But the POINT IS, I HAVE an EXTREMELY IMPORTANT MISSION here. And I VOLUNTEERED for it, KNOWING FULL WELL of the POTENTIALLY ASTRONOMICAL NEGATIVITY which could RESULT from it, both for MYSELF and YOU! But NEVER ONE to REFUSE a PHENOMENAL CHALLENGE, I SIMPLY took it UPON myself. Perhaps PART of my motivation was SELFISH. In fact, NO QUESTION it was. Because I AM a PRETTY SELFISH individual when you get right DOWN to it. Which is WHY I'm now at the PROVERBIAL CROSSROADS here. Actually, not EVEN proverbial, if you THOUGHT about it. But like EVERYTHING I've EVER DONE in life, I'm just going OUT there and having FUN!

Of course, "FUN," in THIS case is QUITE a LOOSE TERM for what I'M having. Because the only WAY I'm going to have ANY fuckin' HOPE of SUCCEEDING is if I can make a fuckin' GAME of it.

After all, LIFE is JUST THAT if you WILL or you WON'T. How's THAT for AWFUL PUNS but GREAT ANALOGIES? But the point IS, the only way I'm GOING to succeed at this ODDS STAGGERING TASK I have BEFORE me, is to STOP myself before I even BEGIN and say, LOOK, DON'T SWEAT IT! Because if you truly FEEL that IT'S ALL EFFORT and NO FUN, then you MIGHT as well NOT EVEN BEGIN!

Because you KNOW that while the BENEFITS of SUCCESS would be FANTASTIC for all CONCERNED, AND THE CONSEQUENCES of FAILURE would be AWFUL for all CONCERNED, the only WAY you're GOING to have ANY fuckin' CHANCE for success, is if you STAY LOOSE and RELAXED, take it one STEP at a TIME, and DON'T WORRY about SETBACKS every now and then.　Because THEY'RE ALL PART of the PLAN, when you get right DOWN to it.

Obviously, I KNEW what I was GETTING myself INTO when I said to my BOSS, PICK ME, I TRULY KNOW I can HANDLE the MOST IMPORTANT fuckin' PROJECT of ALL TIME!　And just so you KNOW, my boss DOESN'T have a PROBLEM with profanity.　And when YOU REALIZE who my boss IS, you may find that SURPRISING.　And you ALSO may SEE MY POINT!

Naturally, the BOSS has EVERY CONFIDENCE in me.　The boss KNOWS that I've HANDLED LOTS of MAJOR projects BEFORE in my life.

But SOMETIMES (and maybe YOU could relate to this), when you SUDDENLY get COCKY and say HEY, LET ME DO THIS THING, I GOT IT COVERED, and the SUPERVISOR says OKAY, GO for it, I BELIEVE in you, and SUDDENLY you fuckin' think, HEY WAIT a MINUTE, DID I just VOLUNTEER for this, FREE and CLEAR, CUT and DRIED?　And THEN you think, OK FUCK, WHAT am I, NUTS?　HOW the FUCK am I GONNA pull it OFF?　Well GUESS

WHAT! That's EXACTLY what I FELT like as SOON as my BOSS gave me the big A-OKAY!

But you KNOW SOMETHING? There's MORE TO it than THAT. A LOT MORE fuckin' TO it. You SEE, if I FUCK UP, there's GOING to be HELL to pay. LITERALLY! Both for ME and YOU! So I SUGGEST YOU THINK about and HARP on that GOOD and HARD, when I COME AROUND and DO what I have to DO.

BEFORE you PUT that BULLET in my HEAD, or KNIFE through my HEART, or BOMB through my BONES. Because you can HURT me ALL you fuckin' WANT to. I'm SO fuckin' DETERMINED to SUC-CEED at this, that YOU can GIVE it your BEST SHOT to STOP me, but I'll just KEEP COMING BACK for MORE. You see, I EXPECT to FEEL MUCH PAIN through my QUEST. And many OTHER agonies TOO. Like SEEING the BLOODSHED of MANY WAR-TORN COUNTRIES, FAMINE, DISEASE, YOU fuckin' NAME IT!

But I've SOME VERY NOTABLE ADVANTAGES going for me, here. For EXAMPLE, IN MY LIFE, I've ALREADY SEEN the MOST HORRIFIC kind of STUFF this fuckin' WORLD has to OFFER. And SO, there's NOTHING so BAD I could SEE NOW that I'M NOT fuckin' USED to ALREADY. That's ONE of my ADVANTAGES. The OTHER is that I'm ALSO like TOTALLY fuckin' INVINCIBLE! Of course, "LIKE," is ACTUALLY the OPERATIVE word HERE. Because I DO HAVE ONE MAJOR fuckin' VULNERABILITY.

I can FEEL PAIN. BIG time.

Now I IMAGINE you'd PROBABLY expect SOMEONE who's DOING what I am to feel NO pain. But the PROBLEM is I, like EVERYONE ELSE in this MISERABLE FUCKIN' WORLD (and I REALIZE I SHOULDN'T ACTUALLY be REFERRING to it as SUCH, but the TRUTH IS I'm JUST VENTING and my BOSS understands), BUT we ALL seem to GET what we DESERVE, and APPARENTLY I'm NO fuckin' EXCEPTION. I mean, when you're STANDING in that INCREDIBLY, ALBEIT PRACTICALLY fuckin' INFINITELY LONG LINE for MISSIONS to VOLUNTEER for which you KNOW are fuckin' NECESSARY, yet you ALSO know ALL TOO WELL of the POTENTIAL DRAWBACKS involved, and by the WAY, though I'd STATED how the MISSIONS were on a VOLUNTEER basis, it DOES NOT MEAN we DON'T get PAID for them if we SUCCEED; the DIFFERENCE, however between OUR MISSIONS and actual JOBS that YOU'RE USED to, are that MUCH MORE DEPENDS on the OUTCOME of our MISSIONS, both GREAT and HIDEOUS.

And of COURSE, this simply MEANS that we get PAID either POSITIVELY or NEGATIVELY depending on whether we SUCCEED or FAIL. So OBVIOUSLY, even though I KNOW I'm going to SUFFER SO FUCKIN' MUCH as I DO MY THING here on EARTH, it will be ABSOLUTELY fuckin' NOTHING compared to how MUCH I'LL SUFFER if I fuckin' FAIL. And like I MAY have INDICATED

BEFORE, YOU'LL ALSO SUFFER IF I FAIL!

So if I were YOU, and YOU HAVE ANY MATERIALS or WEAPONS which HAVE the POTENTIAL to DESTROY the WORLD, or ENOUGH of its LIFE to cause, well how would you say, the END of LIFE as WE fuckin' KNOW IT, I STRONGLY suggest you COOPERATE with ME when I COME AROUND to SEEK them OUT. Because, you see, I HAPPEN to be a PARASITE of sorts. In OTHER words, I CONSUME things. And I can consume ANY TYPE of MATTER there IS. That includes PEOPLE, STEEL, PLUTONIUM, RADIOACTIVE MATERIALS, etc. And just so you know, the QUANTITY doesn't matter EITHER. And I can EVEN consume ALL TOXIC GASES. So if I THINK you're HIDING something on me, I'll just SIMPLY HAVE to start SWALLOWING WHATEVER I FEEL is KEEPING me from FINDING that STUFF, until I DO, and then CONSUME THAT TOO! And if I HAVE to, I'LL CONSUME YOU! Now JUST KNOW that I'LL FEEL ALL SENSATIONS which ACCOMPANY those CONSUMPTIONS INCLUDING ANYTHING EXPLODING or BURNING what was ONCE my BODY. But being I have SO MUCH REPENTING to do to KEEP from GOING to HELL, it's WORTH IT!

Old Point, Old Ball,
My One and All!

Mutuality seems to come in many shapes, substances and sizes. It's neither limited by walls, oceans, fortresses, mountains or great distances. It's only limited by the possible lack of mutual effort on the parts of the individuals it involves to find each other and stay together. In which case, it wouldn't then really be mutuality, would it?

Now if that sounds almost riddle-like to you, then I'm glad. Because in order for this story to really work, you have to be able to appreciate the art of solving a riddle. But, don't worry. Once you've read it — heard it — ingested it into your eternal soul, you'll understand WHY the riddle set-up was so important. But just in case you don't LIKE riddles, and are NOW thinking of abandoning this piece before you go any further, on the premise I've just given you, let me quickly explain that in this story, solving the riddle is the funnest part of reading it. Unless it somehow gets you hooked on the drug, riddlin. Ha. Ha. Sorry. Bad puns and jokes are also thrown into this story for the purpose of my amusement. So if you NOW wish to quit the story, I forgive you. But I'm hoping by THIS juncture, you're already intrigued enough to keep going. And if so, I promise I'll TRY to keep THAT vice to a MINIMUM. Of course, promises were meant to be broken. But if you're still with me, I've a hunch you'll finish. Now to resume.

Myrtle Baines was in the grocery store feeling slightly annoyed. "I must have enough cash on me, but wretchedness is this aggravating," she said to young Johnny, once the boy who used to trample through her yard with his friends which Myrtle had always found adorable. But now he was the more mature cashier who unlike those other boys Myrtle remembered, had decided he'd become a man. And at times like this, she was grateful she'd never felt the need to scold him. "Actually, Johnny, I'm a little short right now," she chuckled embarrassedly, feeling through her blouse pockets as the final alternative after emptying her purse on the counter.

"That's okay, Mrs. Baines. I know you're good for it. Pay me in church or something." What a sweet and understanding young man he'd blossomed.

"Bless you, Johnny. You're one of the most charitable people ever. Tonight when Herb and I say grace over these delicious morsels, you can be sure we'll BOTH put in a delightful word for you to the Lord. And we'll be just as thankful to Him for you, as that blessed meal we'll be able to enjoy because of my faith in Him, and your trust in me." She'd begun to sob a little.

"Take it easy, Mrs. Baines," he said, holding out a rag to her. "You'd do the same for ME. We're like family around here."

Now if that little grocery store scene is enough to enable you to solve the riddle of this story, then by golly, you're as psychic as I. But my guess is that it's not, and quite frankly I KNOW it's not, because like I pointed out in the previous sentence, I'm psychic. And I KNOW you're still up in the air.

But that's GOOD. That's VERY good. Because NOW I can begin to show you how the clues I'm starting to string together for you are going to help you solve the riddle, so you can feel the story was great. Which because I'm psychic, I KNOW you already DO, to this point.

NOW. The 2 clues I'll begin with I've already indicated — #1, I'm psychic, and #2, that scene in the grocery store could NOT have taken place if I WASN'T. Which I KNOW you don't understand. But that's good, that's VERY good. Because now I'll give you some MORE clues until slowly but surely, you'll feel the satisfaction of this story seeping in, like the rush of ink to the back of an EXTREMELY inflated check as YOU sign to cash it. And THAT, was clue #3! HOLY TOLEDO! We're GETTIN' there.

Clues #4 and #5, coming up. Clue #4, this is a very special LOVE story — the kind where 2 who are betrothed to each other are forced to separate until such time as they can reunite. And clue #5, the separation took place in that very grocery store.

Now I know I'd be getting ahead of myself if I gave you any more clues without tying those few together first. SO. Well wait a second, let me just slip in ONE MORE for the moment, and THEN I'll tie them together. How's that sound? Don't worry, it'll WORK. TRUST me. Okay, clue #6, I'M one of the PARTIES in the love story. I know that's the HARDEST clue to digest. But when you think about it, what BETTER kind of love story (which DOES have a happy ending by the way) than one described by a key participant. EH? Oh, wait a second, just ONE more little clue. One more teeny tiny teensy weeney, REAL QUICK! And THEN it's TIE TIME I PROMISE! Okay, clue #7, neither I nor my BETROTHED are one of YOU! Okay?

THERE! That wasn't so bad. Hey, 7 clues. Lucky 7! How can we go wrong, EH? We can't. So sit back, take them all in, and get ready to TIE!

NOW! Given I'm psychic, AND NOT one of YOU, AND I CAUSED a perfectly honest woman buying food in a grocery store to have to steal (well maybe she didn't INTEND to steal, BUT to the best of my knowledge, she STILL hasn't paid young Johnny back yet; well, I take it back, she'll pay him, give her time; it's only been a few days since that occurred), BUT! The point IS, she was ABOUT to write a check for the groceries when she discovered something I CAUSED with my psychic powers (refer to clue #3, if you need to).

Okay then. SO. NOW, you have to do a LITTLE thinking. But don't worry, I'LL bring you through it. Read this passage as carefully as you can and just bear with me. And I'm SURE you'll have figured out

EXACTLY what I did in the grocery store with my psychic powers. And you NEED to, because that's KEY. Not only that, it's important! If Myrtle Baines was about to write a check, okay? You with me so far? Okay. And then SUDDENLY, she's UNABLE to, YET, there's nothing INTERNALLY wrong with her, although she MIGHT have a bout of arthritis from time to time, because she IS rather elderly at this point in her life; HOWEVER! I indicated that she'd turned her purse over on the counter to search for any cash she might have had, and THEN, when she saw there was none THERE, THOROUGHLY searched the pockets of her blouse. AND! In all those acts she committed to which were indicated in that paragraph, she did absolutely NOTHING to indicate she was in any PHYSICAL pain or DISCOMFORT. All she did was state she had no spending cash ON her, and THEN, indicated her GRATITUDE to young Johnny for his CHARITY in FRONTING her the groceries, and THEN, indicated her REMORSE and DISTRESS by SOBBING. SO! This would MEAN something ELSE had made her unable to write that check. Now THINK. In order to write checks, SOMETHING MUST WORK. And if it won't, you CANT.

And while you're harping on THAT, I'M going to do another brief cutaway. And if THIS doesn't indicate what I did to stop Myrtle Baines from writing that check, then I'll just have to take the process of ELIMINATION a step further before we move on. Process of elimination. Good process, GOOD process.

By the way. For THOSE of you who are READING this story to yourselves, ESPECIALLY those with some kind of background in LITERATURE, have you NOTICED I NEVER BREAK my PARAGRAPHS, when I INDICATE a CHANGE of TIME and/or SPACE? Know WHY? I think it's WASTEFUL. After ALL, a story should be COMPACT not SEPARATE. Just MY opinion. Besides, I understand there's a paper shortage. And I should know.

ANYWAY! At the same time Myrtle Baines FAILED to write that check, something else happened in a lawyer's office about 2000 miles away. Stan and Leslie Rumpscott were about to sign some legal papers which would officially annul their brief and bitter marriage. Let's take it from the moment where what should've been their final sentiments as man and wife to each other are spoken.

"You know, Stan, I never imagined this could be the happiest fuckin' day of my life. What did I ever do to deserve you?"

"Just shut up and sign the damn thing, will you?"

"My pleasure! Give me that pen, the LAST thing we'll share."

But as hard as Leslie bore down, the damn thing wouldn't write. "This damn thing won't write! Just like you, Stan, probably never worked a day in its life!"

"Eh, shat up. I've worked harder to deal with YOU, than the builders of the Great Wall, the Leaning Tower and Stonehenge combined!" His eyes seemed to flare as he glared at her.

"Oh, yeah? No wonder those fuckin' places are falling apart."

"Hey, relax, you 2; I've got lots of pens in the office," said Attorney Sylvester, reaching one out to them. "Here."

"Well, thank you very much," said Leslie. "At least there's SOMEONE around here that knows what he's doing." She and Stan exchanged one more dirty look before she tried to sign the paper. "Or, maybe NOT. This pen doesn't fuckin' work, either! Come on, shyster Sylvester, what gives here?"

"Mrs. Rumpscott, could you please curb your tongue a little? I'm sure I can find you a suitable pen."

"Well, you'd better. For the bucks I'm paying you to lose this creep." Stan gave her the finger with a smug grin.

"Feeling's mutual, DICKFACE!"

"Excuse me, can you 2 calm down please? Here's another pen."

But no matter how many pens they tried, none worked. So by the end of the day, the Rumpscotts were still quite married.

Suffice it to say, that could have led to a murder-suicide if MY problem hadn't been solved before too long. OR, should I say, OUR problem, that is, MINE and MY BETROTHED.

Okay, NOW I'll break it DOWN a little here in the mushy-gushy department for you. After all, I'm FEELING kind of mushy-gushy right now about all that's gone on for us lately which is what this story's all about. Now for you humans, the term is EMOTIONAL UNITY. But for US, it's, yeah, that's right, MUSHY-GUSHY! Especially when we get to LEAK together. I know that sounds disgusting, because it indicates we void our wastes together. But THAT'S not the case at ALL. In fact, we don't actually VOID waste in the same sense as YOU do. Of course, we have been known to LEAK from time to time in the PHYSICAL sense, and when we do, that CAN be disgusting. Especially, if we do it in your shirt pockets, all over your hands, or on legally binding contracts, etc. But if we DO, it MEANS there's some kind of psychic message in the INK, from ONE of our units to another. Or maybe more than one psychic message to another of our units. Or maybe ONE psychic message to an ASSORTMENT of units. Or ANY like possible COMBINATION.

Incidentally, have you figured out what we are yet, based on all this stuff? If so indicate it by THINKING it, and we'll move on. What's that? You THINK you have a pretty good idea? COOL! Okay. Then let me NOW begin to unravel for you, exactly what my actions were, my motives for those actions, a GENERAL description of the REST of the CON-

SEQUENCES of my ACTIONS—i.e. the EXCESS BAGGAGE—the WORLDWIDE disturbances—albeit just the BRIEFEST synopsis of THAT stuff, OTHER than what I've ALREADY indicated with Myrtle Baines and the Rumpscotts, and FINALLY the WONDERFUL ENDING to this tale, which would NOT have been POSSIBLE without all my PSYCHIC INTERVENTION.   And I KNOW you're now awaiting THAT with bated breath.

First of all, I'm going to give you a little briefing on the substance, INK.   INK is a SUPERB SUBSTANCE. In fact, much like YOUR BLOOD, it's OUR LIFE FORMULA.   But UNLIKE your blood, it has a very special LOYALTY to EACH and EVERY UNIT it EMBELLISHES. AND the power to transfer itself through INVISIBLE MEANS, from UNIT to UNIT, AS WELL AS, anything or anyone ELSE with the ability to make COGNITIVE DECISIONS! In OTHER words, it's a PSYCHIC MEDIUM.

And what this MEANS is, is that if ANY ONE of us it occupies is in NEED of some kind of ASSISTANCE, it's WILLING and ABLE to cause MANY things to HAPPEN within its REALM.   And for MYSELF and my BETROTHED, it's come through ROYALLY.   So, here's to THEE, oh fabulous INK! My PERSONAL ODE to THEE!   I'm NOW a tad emotional.

Okay, now that I've gotten my stability back (by the way, that's another great thing about ink, it can do a LOT of things that in you HUMANS it takes

DIFFERENT bodily fluids to attain) the only thing it CAN'T do is REPRODUCE, THEREFORE those of us in love, such as Annie and myself, and I'll be Roger for the sake of YOUR simplicity in comprehension, even though those aren't REALLY our NAMES, our ACTUAL names being #ARTS67 and #ARTS68, and THOSE were only TEMPORARY when we rolled off the assembly line together in Algonquin, Texas, or some such place (it TRULY amazes me how you HUMANS are so fuckin' OBSESSED with time, space and names), but ANYWAY, like I was starting to indicate at the beginning of this paragraph, I was getting emotional as I pledged that ODE to INK, and the INK was producing the TEARS, for lack of a better word.

Of course, this would be invisible to you HUMANS, but Annie's right here, and SHE saw, or should I say, IT, yes, that's RIGHT WE'RE both COMPLETELY SEXLESS, and PROUD OF IT, we're just ITS to YOU, yet we can still LEAK together, and none of YOU could ever see that EITHER, as the transference of our INK to each other's BODIES is an ENTIRELY PSYCHIC PROCESS! Obviously, we HAVE bodies.

But INK can EVAPORATE itself as well as it can do everything ELSE it does, and that's JUST what it did in pens WORLDWIDE for a few days, to begin the process of reuniting US, Roger and Annie.

NOW! How did it that REUNITE us, you might wonder. Sure, you wonder, I KNOW, you're ALL on the edge of your SEATS for THIS one. You've reached the part in this story where you sense that everything you've been made to understand so far is so darn CLEVER and THOUGHT PROVOKING, and the writer's a fuckin' GENIUS, go on ADMIT it, you can't HELP it, I'm PSYCHIC, I KNOW what you think, REMEMBER? So here goes, the LONG AWAITED EXPLANATION! In FULL, DEFINITIVE SENTENCES. Just for EVERY ONE OF you ENLIGHTENED HUMANS! I know, you NOW think I'm a fuckin' ASS kisser. Funny you should come up with THAT notion. Why is it funny? Reminds me of a JOKE. A DOCTOR goes into a BANK and WRITES a CHECK using a RECTAL thermometer. When the teller asked him WHY, he said it was because some ASSHOLE HAD HIS PEN, GET IT? If THAT doesn't combine great humor, with MY LIFE STORY, I don't know what does. But I DID promise on the very first PAGE of this tale, I'd TRY to keep the humor to a minimum for you. And I HAVE. The VERY minimum.

ANYWAY. I'm REALLY sorry, I've been prolonging the INEVITABLE JUST to KEEP your INTEREST when I KNOW I'VE had it all ALONG. But NOW the explanations to wrap this story UP. Here goes. REALLY.

Okay, remember back to clue #5 of the 7 I've given you, when I indicated we were separated in that grocery store? Well, the only reason it HAPPENED was we'd been too CARELESS not to ACT.

In other words, Annie and I were so busy LEAKING together (in that psychic, sexless yet most PLEASURABLE way, which I've already INDICATED), and by the way, did I explain how when we DO that, it actually REDUCES our psychic ability a tad, because then our ENERGY for transcranial manipulation is pretty much ZAPPED where you HUMANS are concerned? NO, I guess I hadn't PREVIOUSLY made that CLEAR, but I have NOW, and what that MEANT was when a Doctor Asha Suki of Tokyo's highest rent district (as you humans refer to those regions in your worldwide cities where the average income ranges between 6 and 7 figures a year) had stopped into the grocery store to buy some pasta (what a GOURMET this guy is), and he actually DIDN'T have a PEN on him (go figure that one—I think he'd left his other pen at the lab in nearby Scranton, where he'd been lecturing some American colleagues on the prospect of something called interbinery brain surgery, which of course I know NOTHING about—I only heard it in his thoughts as he took Annie away from me, and onto the plane he had to grab back to Tokyo, after the quick pasta lunch he consumed to make him feel energetic on the flight) as he'd purchased the package of pens Annie and I were in together, but somehow only took Annie, written his check for the pasta, but then left me before I could recover my psychic energy enough to get him to take me too.

So THEN what I needed to do was get young Johnny to take me and MAIL me to Doctor Suki's Tokyo residence as soon as possible. But in order to do that, I HAD to get young Johnny to write down his correct address, of course.

And THERE'S where pen solidarity came in. You see, in order to create a psychic chain long enough for ME to be able to cause a TRANSFER of information like that, from Suki's mind to young Johnny's, I had to rely on the strength of the INK from every PEN in the world. Because while I WAS able to pick up Suki's thoughts when he was within a SHORT distance of me, by the time I figured out what I needed to DO and had gotten ALL of my psychic energy BACK, he was airborne, some 2500 miles away and getting ever FURTHER away, FAR beyond the psychic range of the average pen.

However, when the INK of EVERY pen the world over is in contact, which it always IS, because there's ENOUGH pens and/or OTHER appliances that use ink, printing presses, blotters, etc., so that the psychic range between EACH can't exceed ANY distance, at LEAST thank GOODNESS, not between myself and Annie; HOWEVER, in order for a mission of THIS magnitude to be undertaken and ACHIEVED, the INK of all those PENS has to work TOGETHER in an EVAPORATED STATE, because IN that state, the psychic bond between OURSELVES AND any HUMANS we need to MANIPULATE is MAXIMIZED.

So as a result, or RESULTS, as there were quite a few of those stemming from ink in every pen around the globe suddenly evaporating for the sake of bringing Annie and I together again, which happened just before young Johnny, who was able to receive Doctor Suki's address in his mind through ME from the psychic chain which had occurred when the combined aforementioned effort of all those pens bloomed to fruition. Naturally, at THIS point, Annie and I were the only working pens on earth (and by the WAY, though I'm HOPING YOU had SOLVED the riddle of this story at LEAST a good 7 pages ago, about us being PENS, because as I'd indicated on the FIRST page, that was the funnest part of READING the story, since other than THAT, there are really no unusual twists and turns in the plot, except for the FALLOUT it had on the REST of the world, which I'll get to SHORTLY, but ANYWAY, if you really weren't SURE BEFORE about the answer to the riddle, I've NOW given you the answer VERBATIM, which means you have NO excuse for not KNOW-ING it by NOW, other than IGNORANCE or ILLITERACY) and like I was starting to indicate before those last parentheses, Annie and I were the only working pens on the planet for a few days. Which means the LAST thing WRITTEN before the crisis ENDED was Doctor Suki's address by young Johnny through ME on a small envelope whose destination was MY BLISS!

Naturally, Annie had everything under control

on the other end. With Annie's psychic strength, Doctor Suki's actions were limited to simply leaving Annie in a drawer in his house, after he got home, and of course, Annie KNEW through the psychic pen chain around the world that I was on my way. (Remember, Annie and I are ITS, not HE and SHE — AH, EQUALITY, HOW GLORIOUS IT IS!) Anyway that's NOW our SPECIAL DRAWER, and our PERMANENT DREAM HOME! And Doctor Suki's SO WONDERFUL to us. He leaves us alone most of the time, NEVER takes us when he LEAVES his HOUSE, ONLY uses us when he has to take a quick NOTE, PHONE message, new idea diagram for brain surgery, THAT sort of stuff. And he SURE IS a THINKING man. His thoughts are more complex than every Sony and microchip unit he's got IN there. And what a connoisseur of GREAT MUSIC and a WONDERFUL CHEF he is. Annie and I LOVE the sounds and smells all around. And what a NEAT freak. Of course, we KNOW he won't MARRY. His career is EVERYTHING. Of course, as I'd INDICATED, there was SOME fallout from the PEN crisis. Some GOOD — schoolchildren got to MISS homework, some suicides were AVERTED as potential victims couldn't write NOTES and thought BETTER of it. But some bad — DEATHS from unwritten prescriptions, potential economic collapse, etc. But it's over now. And Annie and I feel MIGHTIER than Suki's Samurai swords.

Spinaround

S andy prepared the lasagna using the spicy Cajun recipe she learned while working as a maid in New Orleans. Its saucy crust was enhanced by the red peppers and black-eyed peas she'd added. As she slid the pan into the oven, she couldn't help notice how the extra ingredients seemed to form a face much like her own.

A lump filled her throat as she closed the oven door. She hummed Swanee, because it always lifted her spirits. Somehow she felt her life must have been improving. After all, here she was finally up North with a nice job, away from the prejudice and mammy jokes. What's more, she was with her man and child. It was just a matter of keeping the faith. Everything would soon be wonderful. After all, she'd always been good to everyone, and she truly believed reaching her full potential was inevitable.

Greta, the head chef was filleting a pork roast. Sandy both admired her efficiency, and wondered about her. Aside from working hard and being firm yet fair, Greta's life was quite the mystery. It was comforting for Sandy to have a boss who wouldn't suddenly snap at her for no reason.

"Need any help, Greta?"

Greta looked up and sniffed. "Sure smells flavorful, San."

Sandy smiled and shook her head, grateful for the compliment.

"Just how many awards did you win down there around Dixieway?" This was a side of Greta Sandy had never seen. And although she found it flattering, she didn't know how to react.

"Oh, no, Greta, nothing like that. I just won a blue ribbon at a country bake-off once but...."

"Come on, Sandy. Don't be so modest, girl. Your Creole cooking's sure to give Sarno's top billing from every restaurant critic in town." She fluttered her eyelashes with sincerity.

"Why thank you, Greta. But you still didn't answer my question. Do you need any help?"

"Just keep cooking like you're cooking and that's all the help I'll need, okay?" Greta was again giving full attention to the roast.

Sandy now wondered if she'd offended her. Yet there was no point in pushing it since things were still going well.

"Sure, Greta. Thanks."

Orders were soon coming in left and right. Sandy felt somewhat proud of herself, since her addition to the restaurant added tasty options for the customers. And with enough hard work, maybe someday she'd have her own place. But she now wanted nothing more than to feel respectable.

Sandy liked when it got busy. She always worked well under pressure, especially with the type of acknowledgment Greta had just given her, which she felt was way too infrequent with everyone in her life. And for awhile she was able to stop thinking of her hardships, with those sorrowful feelings gone for the moment.

She imagined herself back in the newly liberated South, celebrating the sudden freedom with all her kin. Maybe she lived back then. She could feel her creativity busting the chains that bound her. She loved hard work and being productive, but on her own terms.

Wrapped up in the sounds of people working, eating and enjoying themselves, it took a moment to notice Greta's exasperation as she handed her the phone. Would this never end? "Please keep it brief, okay?"

Her world seemed frozen in time. Why did he have to do this? It was so unfair.

"When will you be home?" Sandy could almost smell the alcohol on his breath, his voice low and raspy.

"When I'm through here! Look, Kyle, I might lose my job." She tried to speak softly so she wouldn't be noticed, hoping he'd stay calm.

"Why can't you be home cooking? You take better care of your customers than you do me!"

She quickly changed the subject to try to offset his self-pity. "Is Andy sleeping?" The usual moment of silence. "Kyle. What about Andy?"

He'd obviously been celebrating the union strike again by guzzling at Nathan's with a few of his trucker cronies. But far be it for her to bring that up.

"Don't worry about Andy. He's got no problems. The sitter gave him his formula and now he's crashing on cloud 9. Isn't he lucky, Sandy? He's got a daddy who loves him. But is his mother around at 5:30 at night? She's supposed to be.."

"Come on, Sandy, you're starting to fall behind."

"Sorry, Greta. Kyle, I've got to go now. See you later."

"No! No! Don't hang up! Every night it's the same damn—"

Sandy forced down the phone, dreading the moment. With any luck, he'd now go to sleep and be passed out on the couch by the time she got home. Otherwise....

"Sandy, everything okay?" She made herself smile and nodded.

"All right then. Get back to work." It was hard not to cry.

Being between a rock and a hard place was Sandy's life story. But it'd always made her stronger and she was determined as ever.

In spite of what was happening now, she still felt Kyle was the best thing to ever come her way. After all, he relieved her of that unpleasant employment in the French Quarter by cutting Madame H'Ouvre down to size (just where she belonged), and then his sudden midnight rescue. Fate must've played a role, since what odds of his truck breaking down at the estate of perhaps the most prominent landowner below the Mason-Dixon line—directly descended from one of Thomas Jefferson's secret lovers—for whom it was rumored the state of Louisiana had been purchased.

She'd had the time of her life on the road with Kyle for 6 months. So they drove 9 hours a day, ate all their meals at greasy spoons and slept in the seat, under the shelter of the highway moon. He was the sweetest man in the world, and the first person to ever make her feel human. He sang love songs to her accompanied by the radio voices of Hank Williams, Ernie Ford or whatever other country bumpkin helped him express himself. He wrote her poetry right there in the truck, as she lay asleep in his arms, which he gently woke her to each morning, when it was time for them to move on. He bought her flowers at rest stops, whenever he could. But most of all, he told her never to give up on her dream of being a self-made woman, and that he'd help her every step of the way, through good times and bad.

She realized it was a mutual thing, and right now he was the one who needed support and understanding. After all, he'd taken a gamble by settling up here to keep his route local so they could find a place to raise Andy, and she could work her trade. The U.S. interstates were certainly no place for a child to grow up. Unfortunately, it turned out to be a more demanding area for his career, as trucker strikes were much more common at the local level.

And with his patience tried like this, he often turned to the bottle for relief, but Sandy knew Kyle still loved her and Andy, and really wanted things to work out.

She was back in the swing of things for the moment, yet Greta's look of concern for her could not be ignored. "I want to talk to you when we have a minute." Sandy nodded, realizing the situation with Kyle was a part of her life she'd have to deal with publicly. Sometimes he'd call 2 or 3 times on any evening before settling in, but if he did now, she'd refuse to take it. This was the only way he'd learn. But what more did she need to learn?

The last hues of sunset through the window reminded her of the many nights when they stopped along the road to rest. It also reminded her of the night they'd met, and she finally broke down. "That's it. I'm finished here. What's the use in trying to explain this away." The busboy noticed her first and looked like he wanted to help but didn't know what to say. So Sandy continued to work the best she could, but within seconds all the kitchen help was looking at her. It seemed ironic that with everything going on, Greta was the last one to notice.

"All right, Sandy. Time out. Minna, cover for me for a few minutes, okay?" Greta put an arm around her and led her gently into the back room. After grabbing her some tissues, she held her and didn't speak until Sandy was finished.

"Look, I'm not going to ask if you're okay, because you're obviously not. But what we need to figure out is how to deal with it. Now you don't have to tell me the problem; I know it's Kyle."

Sandy nodded slowly, like the perpetrator of a centuries-old mystery finally realizing the jig was up. And as she stood there beside the woman to whom she seemed to bear her soul, the comfort of her empathy was welcome relief.

But she wanted to be careful and say the right things, so as not to give the wrong idea about Kyle, or her life at home. Otherwise, she knew it would jeopardize everything she'd worked so hard for.

"Thanks, Greta. It's really nice to be able to open up."

"I'm just going to ask you right out. Does he hit you?" Was it that obvious? After all, it's not like he did it all the time. Besides, with her dark, brazen complexion it was pretty easy to cover with a little makeup.

"He loves me, Greta. But things have been tough for him of late. You know he's out of work, and when he's frustrated, he drinks for recreation. Maybe it's to help him forget, I don't know." She knew there was no point in rambling on, since Greta had already figured it out. "He's really a great guy when he's sober. And he'd never really hurt me. But sometimes at night when I come home he can be a little rough, but it's only because he isn't used to not working, and me not being there, and when he's drunk, all his inner feelings come out in one lump sum."

"That's his excuse. Now what's yours for staying with him?"

This question seemed as hard hitting as anything he'd ever done to her. But it was impossible for Sandy to be mad, since she felt such a purge at being able to discuss this for the first time. She only hoped it wouldn't come back to haunt her.

"He's the father of my child, Greta. And the most blessed event in my life to this point. How can you even ask that?"

"Because I've been there! And while I'm sure you've probably heard this cliché a million times, it WILL only get worse!"

Her speculation aside, Sandy now wondered how bad Greta had gotten it. After all, she seemed a pretty strong-willed woman. But this was no time to try to learn her life story. Although she was beginning to see Greta as a friend as well as a boss, it was sad how it took her own abuses to make this happen. In that sense, it was very much like the way she and Kyle had begun.

"But what am I supposed to do? I want our son to be raised by his 2 natural parents, and not end up having to be carted around to lots of foster homes with a bunch of half-siblings like I was, you know? Right now, Kyle and Andy are the only family I got, at least whose whereabouts I'm sure of."

Greta looked strained with surprise. "You mean

you don't know where anyone is you left down there?"

"Not really. The only one I 'm pretty sure about is an uncle I have in Tennessee, but he was...." Greta nodded in understanding. "Of course, he probably knows where some of my brothers and sisters are at, considering how we were all his playthings at one time. But it probably would take a command from God for the bastard to give me that information."

Greta took her hand. "I'm sorry, Sandy. Let's get back to work now. But know if there's anything I can ever do, just say what." Sandy felt another restoration in her life was at hand.

While her future was dominated by anxiety and confusion, at the moment she felt on top of things. As the workshift continued, everyone around her seemed to be smiling like they were in her corner, though she'd hardly spoken to anyone there since she'd taken the job a few weeks earlier. She was a woman of few words, who's small talk skills were limited, and believed action was the best form of communication. Even with Kyle and Andy, there'd never been much talking, other than moments of passionate affection, or lately in her case, anguish and pain.

It wasn't long before she heard rumbling in the dining room. She realized it was Hank, the doorman in conversation with a loud patron. The words were muffled at first, but soon there was no mistaking what he said. "I'm sorry, sir. You can't go back there. Employees only." Then with the cry of the baby, she knew who was out there.

"Oh, my God, I don't believe it." She peeked through the window in the door, and sure enough, there was Kyle with Andy in his arms. He'd sat down at a table, and was trying to calm him back to sleep.

"I'm sorry, sir," he said to Hank, in his usual apologetic manner. "I didn't know he'd wake up. I just wondered if his mama wanted to say hi to him. At least now, she can cook for me."

Sandy wondered if many people were staring at him. She also looked around the kitchen to see if anyone seemed aware of the commotion. It wasn't like people were falling all over each other to find out what happened, for which she was grateful. At least for the moment, the scene was over.

But with the initial embarrassment behind her, Sandy now had to think of Kyle and Andy's well-being. Kyle was in no condition to drive, and bringing Andy here like this had endangered their lives. So she was now faced with the responsibility of calling them a cab, on top of all her other duties. And that would surely lead to another confrontation later on. She hoped he planned to eat something, which would at least absorb some of the alcohol. Then again, maybe she'd be better off if he were removed from the premises out cold.

"Greta. You know how you said you wanted to help me?" She thought she might've come across as sarcastic but at times like this she had trouble sounding civil.

"Sure." Not that she knew it would do any good.

"Try to keep an eye on table 12. And be ready to call 911." Sandy said this to make Greta aware of how bad for business Kyle could be. That way Greta wouldn't feel she was sacrificing her own responsibilities for Sandy's sake.

"You mean he's out there?" Sandy nodded. Of course, there was really little chance he'd get violent in the restaurant. Not at the cost of disturbing Andy. But the fact he'd brought him to Sarno's in this drunken state indicated his behavior was already becoming more erratic.

Greta was peeking out through the door. "Sandy, your baby's adorable. He has that same expression of independence you have. Like he knows what he wants in life, and is willing to do whatever it takes to get it. Even in his sleep." Sandy had never heard her son described this way, and found it very enlightening.

"Thanks. But what's Kyle doing?" It was such a shame this kind of moment had to be so bittersweet.

"He's holding and swaying him gently. If you want, I'll tell Hank to get him a high chair." This seemed like another possible dilemma. Andy always slept much better lying down, and he still only took formula, so it wasn't like he'd be eating anything.

"I know what. Can you see if someone has a quilt he can lie on? That way if Kyle orders something, Andy can rest comfortably on the table. In the meantime, I'm going to have to break free for a few seconds to call them a cab. Believe me, Greta, he's in no condition to be behind the wheel."

"Sure, girl. See what I can do." Greta patted Sandy's back.

For awhile everything went okay. Greta found Andy a quilt and Kyle ordered the "all you can eat special," which Sandy had already made famous in her short time there. And while he dined, she was able to call for the cab, telling the driver to come and wait for his charge at Sarno's, and that he could leave the meter running while he did so. After all, it was most important he be there when Kyle was ready to leave, since there was no telling when that would be.

Unfortunately, Kyle also ordered a few beers. And while it was Sarno's policy to try to keep its customers from driving under the influence, they hadn't known what it was to encounter anyone like him. It didn't take them long to find out.

"Check please. Check please! I'm all done. Everything was great! But I've got to get home now! My baby needs his rest. And I don't want to miss my woman when she comes home. She works here, you know! And let me tell you all, she's one fine...."

"Excuse me, sir. Can you please be a little quieter. People are trying to relax and enjoy their meals."

By now everyone's attention was centered around Kyle, with Sandy beside herself. This was her worst experience since the night Madame H'Ouvre had threatened to whip her before a group of dignitaries because she'd made their mousse too rich. She wanted someone to tell Hank the cab was waiting. She also hoped Kyle's waitress wasn't too taken aback. Later she'd have to explain the situation to her, and why Kyle wasn't expected to tip her very much, though she probably deserved 50% for what she put up with.

It wasn't long before someone had told the cabbie to come in. He approached Kyle. "I'm here to take you and your child home."

Kyle stood up and looked around in a dazed manner, like he couldn't yet accept the fact he'd created a conspiracy against himself. "What are you talking about, I don't need no chauffeur. I brought my own wheels." The cabbie looked at Hank with hope. Now it was his turn to try to make Kyle understand.

"Excuse me, Kyle is it?" Hank said. Kyle nodded slowly, his expression defensive. "Well, Kyle, you're simply in no shape to be operating a motor vehicle tonight. And since your wife, Sandy is an employee here, and that's her infant son you have, it's my responsibility to see that he gets home safely."

"First of all, mister, Sandy ain't my wife, she's

my lady in waiting. And second of all, he's my baby, too. And I brought him here in one piece, and I can get him home in one piece."

But Hank had a surprise for him. "Sir, I'm afraid your car's been towed. You can get it tomorrow." Kyle lashed out at him.

Hank and the cabbie were eventually able to subdue him. But not before a few glasses were broken, some silverware was knocked to the floor, and several customers had left without ordering anything.

When the fight began, Sandy had immediately come out of the kitchen to make sure Andy was okay. She never really believed Greta would have to call 911, even though she'd told her to be ready. Andy was unhurt, and amazingly had stayed asleep through the whole incident.

When police arrived, Kyle surrendered to them without a struggle. He chose to spend the night in jail over being driven home. Sandy found it amazing how every ounce of his selfish pride was brought out by the alcohol. In addition to being disorderly, Kyle also faced the possibility of assault charges if Hank or the cabbie chose to press them.

"Is this what you want this beautiful son of yours to grow up with?" said Greta, as she cradled Andy in her arms near closing time. "Heck, if this kind of stuff keeps up, he may not even get to grow up. He could've been killed tonight! I don't think I can overemphasize the dramatic quite enough."

Sandy had a difficult time pondering this. But she knew she'd probably find it in her heart to forgive Kyle as she always had.

"Well at least now I know he's not cheating on me." This was the best Sandy could come up with to lighten the moment. Greta shook her head, unmoved by Sandy's attempt to shrug it off.

"He's spending the night in the hoosegow! And all because he couldn't be man enough to let you have your livelihood. The way I see it, he's depriving you of your chance to be well and prosper. If that isn't cheating, I don't know what is!"

Andy gurgled and stretched. Sandy admired him in Greta's arms, seeing Kyle's good side in the fact he looked so healthy and happy, despite all else. So Andy spent most of the day with the sitter, who took care of all his infant essentials. No matter what happened from here on, she felt Andy was going to be fine. Because if she had to, she'd keep Andy with her all the time when Kyle shirked his parental responsibilities. And Kyle would understand, after what happened tonight. He always felt bad later on about his shenanigans, after he sobered up. And now Sandy knew keeping Andy at the restaurant wouldn't be a problem. Everyone loved her cute little boy, giving formula was easy, and diapers could be changed quickly. Things were going to be all right.

"I know it's been a long day," said Sandy, bent on putting it behind her without further discussion.

"And I'm ready to go."

The next morning when Sandy went to bail him out, he didn't seem to remember much. At least of what had really happened. "Honest, Sandy, I remember coming home, checking Andy in his crib, then calling the dispatch to see if Homer wanted us on the picket line today. And when I found out he did, I decided to go out, grab a pizza and turn right in so I'd be bright-eyed and bushy tailed."

Sandy just looked at him in disbelief. She didn't know what hurt more, the fact he didn't remember her cooking for him, or his blatant disregard for Andy's safety and her feelings. She was either dealing with a man completely out of control, or a pathological liar. But what difference did it make?

"I don't know about you anymore," she said, while she drove them home. "If you don't get some kind of help, I think I'll...."

"I know, you're right, honey," he said, putting his arm around her. "When I wake up in the big house, and my sweet woman has to come down to get me and pay my way out, with our precious little child. And now I'm already late for the line."

Sandy felt what seemed like sincerity surge from him as she floored the car in the other direction. "Hey, Sandy, where you going? This ain't the way home."

"I'll drive you to the dispatch. For my own peace of mind."

Sandy felt her assertiveness growing. It was

time to start laying things on the line for him, and this was the first step. "But how am I going to get home later after picket duty?"

"Oh, I don't know, Kyle. Maybe Homer, Chuck or Sid will provide you with transportation. Hey, if they were real friends, they'd be nice enough to find you a designated driver after they got blitzed with you. Or who knows, maybe the strike will settle this very day. And you can actually be back to work by tomorrow. If not sooner." Sandy now believed he preferred this new lifestyle to his job.

"That's ridiculous! Do you have any idea how far apart labor and management are today? The strike probably won't end for at least a couple of months." She dreaded hearing this. "But don't worry, Sandy; I'm not going to drink with them anymore." Yeah, right. "So let's go home so I can get my car."

"Your car isn't home, sweetie. It was towed from Sarno's last night. But I guess you don't remember that, either."

"Oh, my God! What else happened?"

"Not much. You assaulted one of my co-workers and a cab driver. But don't worry. They told me they wouldn't press charges. Now let's see, what else. You took care of Andy like he was an egg. But he still loves his daddy, don't you, sweetie."

Kyle shook his head. "Wow! That's so un-believable."

At this point Sandy had doubts about her own

reality. It almost seemed like she was being put to some kind of test by God, or any other deity she could've been unknowingly indebted to.

As a child, she went to church regularly because every foster home she was raised in was dominated by God fearing adults. And she learned to appreciate this in later life, as she felt the need to fall back on something for guidance. Even while in the employ of Madame H'Ouvre, she found a black church in the community she snuck off to every once in awhile. Of course Madame H'Ouvre believed God made niggers for servitude, so they had no say in their own destinies. It was this kind of thinking, and Sandy's priorities for survival which had steered her away from organized religion.

But she now wondered if these recent occurrences were a sign for her to seek God's understanding and forgiveness.

After all, she hadn't prayed or gone to confession in at least 3 years. Then to bear a child out of wedlock, and continue to have non-marital relations. It was considerable.

"Kyle. What would you think of marrying me?" The uncertainty with which she asked this was outweighed by a sense of morality.

"Why don't we see on that. In the meantime, I want my car."

That settled that. Sandy knew it was important to take every necessary precaution against this man. And if he really loved her, he'd understand.

"Your car's across town at some garage."

Kyle moaned in frustration, like his being upset without a temper loss was the hardest but most necessary challenge he'd ever have to face. "Well, would you mind telling me which one?"

Sandy felt an idea developing. It was a long shot, but it could prove pivotal in the mending of their relationship.

"You know, if you thought about it, you might see this as a helpful predicament." Not likely.

"What the hell are you talking about?"

"Well, since you're already late for the picket line, and I don't have to work until tonight, why don't I pick you up and bring you home lat—"

"Oh, come on, Sandy!"

"Kyle! Please, just hear me out on this. If you really want to prove your love to me." She tried to look sideways into his eyes, without taking her own off the road. Finally, he sighed his acceptance.

She continued. "Just for a couple of days. Because this way no matter what, the chance to drink and drive won't be there."

She paused for a few seconds to let the idea sink in. Of course, this still left much to chance, like whether or not he'd continue to drink and abuse her even if he wasn't able to drive for a few days. And even if he agreed to hold out, what about afterward. Then again, every long journey began with a single step, and Sandy still had enough faith in his intentions to trust him this much. Otherwise, she would've left him at the lock-up.

He finally took her hand. "Okay, babe, you got yourself a deal. After all, I guess I got off easy, because if I really done all that stuff they said and also got caught driving, the cops would've lifted my license for who knows how long. And then I wouldn't even be able to work when the strike was over."

His logic surprised her like a revelation. If this wasn't a super sign of things to come, she didn't know what was. She felt like calling Greta to brag about what a great man she really had after all.

"I love you, Kyle. More than anyone in the world." The morning seemed fresh and alive to her, like the way it did when the sun came up the day after he took her away from that hell hole where she'd been indentured.

"I love you just as much. And now I'll help you love yourself." Sandy had never believed him more.

She made sure the house was stocked full of food for him. If he was truly committed to this deal, Kyle would make the effort. After all, she'd taught him a few things about kitchen work since they'd been settled.

And she'd have to miss her afternoon soaps. But since her own life was becoming a real one, it was well worth the sacrifice.

Besides, the sitter would get the day off, since Andy would be with her until she left him at home with Kyle that evening. Which would save them a few bucks, and that was always good for keeping the peace.

As it turned out, the day couldn't have gone better. Kyle was waiting for her at the dispatch smiling and sober by 3:30. As they were a little early when they got home, it led to some of the best lovemaking they'd ever had. And Sandy had never gone to work feeling better.

But when she arrived, Greta looked mad as hell. Sandy had no idea what she was steamed about, but didn't want to say hello, fearing it could set her off. She couldn't recall when she'd ever seen her like this, and before she knew it, Sandy was pretty nervous. Because with all the happenings of late, the last thing she needed was to be around a ticking time bomb. And after the workshift started, she soon discovered her fear was justified.

"Sandy, get in here!" Greta indicated the back room. Unlike last night, there'd be no sympathy or understanding. Only an unmistakably important message to get across.

"When are you going to lose that asshole?" Sandy felt like she'd been hit with an emotional tidal wave. There was no way to answer this one without falling to pieces. So she simply broke off eye contact with Greta to let the chips fall where they may.

"I had quite the run-in with Mr. Johnson this morning! He'd heard about last night. And he told me to fire your ass, as soon as you got here today." Sandy had never actually met Sarno's owner, but remembered seeing him when she'd submitted her résumé. But now that seemed a foregone conclusion. "But I told him, no check that, I IMPLORED him to let it slide this one time. I reminded him of what an excellent chef you are. And how hard you work. But last night, with that little episode, several of our best customers walked out of here without buying any food! Because of that little episode! And as Mr. Johnson pointed out, no matter how good you are, or how hard you work, bottom line, paying customers. Otherwise, no business, right?" Sandy wished she'd just get this over with. "So I pointed out these people should understand the problem and come back. Give her another chance. But was that enough? No, Sandy. So now MY ass is on the line! For YOU! Because of HIM! Capice?"

Sandy wasn't sure what she was getting at, but it was obvious there'd been a reprieve which depended on a very delicate balance between friendship and subordination. It soured her heart to think Greta may have taken it personally, although she was quite grateful for whatever conditions were about to be disclosed. They sure bested the possibility she'd dreaded a few seconds earlier.

"What exactly are you saying, Greta?" Greta untightened her face a little, as if she'd realized it was pointless to explain this in anger.

"What I'm saying is, is if that wonderful boy-friend of yours ever so much as sets foot in this establishment again, we're both out on our asses!

And as fond as I've already grown of Andy, he'd better not ever again be brought into this kitchen. Mr. Johnson made that crystal clear, and believe me there are people in this place who spy for him, like if they kiss his ass, he'll kiss theirs, you know what I mean?"

Sandy was once again at a loss for words. She wanted to make sure Greta knew how thankful she was for her sacrificing her own job security. At the same time, she knew Greta was still her boss, and now one wrong or misconstrued statement could lead to her termination. Not to mention any future episode with Kyle. "You may find this hard to believe," began Sandy, after a moment of reflection and rationalization, "but I think Kyle's turned over a new leaf." It was the wrong thing to say.

"You know what, you're such a fuckin' jerk! How you're able to complain about people who've treated you badly or molested you completely boggles the mind. At least you've always had someone to take care of you. Even that plantation lady who was so terrible paid you some pretty good nest-egg money. Why don't you just count your damn blessings while you can, and realize you've got a million options?"

Greta's barrage was felt full force and Sandy wanted to retreat without firing back. Otherwise the consequences could be devastating. The trick was to maintain her self-control and show the white flag without doing more damage.

"Is it okay if we get back to work now?" She tried to sound as meek and show as little expression as possible. Greta glared at her for a few more seconds before indicating she could do so.

The remainder of the workshift passed without incident. Yet throughout it Sandy felt the tension everywhere. It was like the battle had ended, but she was still very much in the minefield, knowing full well many forces were about which could set it off. When it was finally time to go, she'd never felt more relieved.

As she drove home, Sandy tried to figure out whether Greta's tirade had been out of disgust for the way she'd let Kyle abuse her, or because she'd actually felt Sandy had it better than she did. Of course, the reason could've simply been Greta was upset over having her job put on the line. But Sandy had a hunch there was more to Greta than meets the eye, and hoped someday it would be possible she could really get to know her.

To this point, it seemed like every person in Sandy's life had somehow ended up turning on her. Even if they hadn't meant to. From the beginning, with her parents' abandonment of each other during their teen years, which led to several combinations of half-siblings from each of them, since their hormones were still running wild for other people. And even after she'd been grouped with them by the state into several foster homes, all of which would give them away saying they were out of control, after uncle Mike had fondled their love away, none of them ever wanted to keep in touch with her. She figured it wasn't personal, they probably just had goals and dreams of their own to pursue, and those sorrowful memories of early life would get in the way. So Sandy was now convinced more than ever after Madame H'Ouvre and Kyle how the trust and love of a true friend was something she'd never really experienced. She hoped Greta could fill that void.

Because even with the reprimand and the harsh words, Greta had already shown she really cared about her. And the more Sandy thought about it, the more she believed Greta hadn't a jealous bone in her body, and her being upset was either out of concern for her or a cry for help of her own. Or maybe both. In any case, she'd no doubt by tomorrow night after Greta had the time to cool off and think it through, things would be good between them again. And it warmed her heart.

As she turned the corner up her street, Sandy noticed a bunch of parked care she'd never seen. At first this didn't bother her. Then she saw the trail of them led right into her driveway.

"Oh, no! What the hell's going on? All the lights are on! And that loud music! There's no way Andy could be sleeping through this!"

Anger and fear were never more present. This could've been the most preventable trap she'd ever fallen into. But because of Andy it was too late to do anything but go in and bear the worst.

She ran with her fists clenched from where she'd parked by the apartment next door. It was amazing the police hadn't been called. This was a quiet, residential neighborhood and that's why they'd come to terms with the realtor in the first place. She was almost inclined to run and call them herself, but for the time. Her maternal instinct told her to get to Andy as soon as possible. Whatever Kyle's response would be to her disapproval of these goings on, she was a lot stronger than Andy, and had to make sure he was okay at all costs.

"Hey, good lookin,' what ya got cookin," Kyle and his buddies bellowed to the song they'd cranked up on the stereo, as she flew in the door. "Hey! And speaking of good lookin,' look who's here, my wonderful old lady. A toast, gentlemen. To my wonderful old lady." They all raised their beer bottles. "Here, here."

"Where's Andy, you buffoon?" She could hear him cry loudly, and wasted no time in running to his bedroom, but didn't find him in the crib. She ran hysterically into every room on the ground floor, before she realized his noise was coming from the cellar. She nearly tripped on the stairs going down.

He was rolling around beside the washing machine, his excrement seeped out on the floor. "Oh, no!" She picked him up and removed his ruined diaper. She wanted to try to console him, but knew it was pointless until he was cleaned, changed and fed.

The key was to stay calm, and handle this without losing her head. She brought him upstairs to the bathroom sink, covering his ears from the music as best she could. Finally, after washing his behind with a warm cloth, she put him down and ran into the den.

Big mistake. But there was no way she couldn't confront Kyle.

"What the hell did you do to Andy, that I found him lying in his own shit down the cellar?" screamed Sandy, as she shut the stereo off.

"Hey, put that back on! That's our cowboy music. It isn't every nigger gets to feel like a real cowboy." Kyle stood up and headed toward her while his guests quietly began to confirm the seriousness of the situation amongst themselves.

"Answer me, Kyle! Or I swear I'll bust every fuckin' record in this room!" She picked up several LPs from off the deck and held them high in the air.

"I don't know what you're talking about! The only time I was down the cellar was when I did a wash a few hours ago. If you weren't so damn useless, you'd do the laundry around here like a real old lady's supposed to! Then you'd know where Andy was at all times!"

Totally enraged, she threw the records across the room with all her might. Kyle's fist landed hard and fast against her right cheek knocking her back, as Andy began screaming.

Though she couldn't see very well through the oozing blood on her face, Sandy was able to kick an ottoman into him which toppled him. Then she ran to grab Andy, and fled out the door.

"Come back here with my son, you ho, you cunt!" Fortunately she had enough steps on him to make it to her car, before he was able to catch up. And as she sped away, wiping her bleeding face with her sleeve as best she could, she realized how smart she'd been in convincing him to leave his towed car at that garage.

Andy continued to cry as Sandy drove along. She cuddled him in her lap, knowing her first stop before the police station was the drugstore. There she'd buy formula, diapers and gauze pads for her face. It wasn't until the clerk asked her if she was okay, when the idea of being homeless with a 5 and a half week-old child really grabbed her.

"No! No, I'm not okay." She kept a look out on Andy in the front seat with the gauze pad she had pressed tight against her cheek. As important as his needs were right now, there was no way she could tend to them with her blood all over him.

"Would you like to use the phone, miss?" The young man's concern was overshadowed by the little time there was to act. The sooner the restraining order was obtained, the better off she and Andy would be. And there was still the matter of Andy's needs to be met first.

"Thanks. But I'm in a big hurry." As she finally drove off, Sandy wished she could've seemed a little more gracious to him.

She was thankful the cut wasn't any deeper, otherwise she'd be driving to the hospital for stitches. But Greta's message was now felt loud and clear, and no matter how sorry Kyle was this time, it would never be enough.

Sandy recognized one of the police officers from earlier in the day, when she'd bailed out Kyle. She wished she could've been there last night when Kyle was brought in so the desk sergeant would recognize her. Obviously, this wasn't the same one who'd been there in the morning.

She felt amazingly calm as she explained the situation to him. Andy had quieted down and this made things much easier for her.

"Were there witnesses to the attack, Ms. Arthur?" This could present an immediate problem, since they were all friends of Kyle's. But it was important for her to be truthful and patient. "Yes. But I wouldn't count on them for much help. I don't suppose there's a way you guys could find knuckle prints in my cheek." He chuckled and shook his head.

"No, ma'am, there isn't. But if he has a history of being violent to you, I'm sure getting a restraining order won't be a problem. An arrest, however requires a little more evidence."

"Sergeant, he was brought in last night. For

assault!"

The sergeant was checking the docket. "Well ma'am, according to this, Kyle Samuelson was arrested last night. But then all the charges were dropped and he was released this morning. It would have been much easier for all concerned if he were still in our custody." Sandy knew that more than ever.

"But he hit me. Don't you see the gash on my face?" Despite the unfairness of the situation, she wasn't going to lose her cool.

"Yes, and maybe he did, ma'am. But unless you can prove he did it, I'm afraid we can't bring him in. Now if there were witnesses...." He raised his right hand, in indication he figured she knew how American justice worked.

But for the time being, Sandy figured she should merely be content with the restraining order. "I see. In that case, let's just get the restraining order out of the way, so I can find me and Andy a bed somewhere. We're both pretty tired."

"Fine. Do you know anyone who's ever witnessed his violent behavior toward you?" It almost seemed like she was the one who might as well have to face criminal charges.

"Yes, sergeant. Anyone who works with me at Sarno's. And the cab driver who came to take him home from there last night." It was now hard for her to keep from raising her voice a little.

"All right, Ms. Arthur, I know it's late, and it's

hard to disturb people at this hour. But I'm afraid I'll need some kind of verbal account from a third party about his violent behavior toward you to obtain that restraining order. Can you think of anyone in particular you can call to verify this?"

This had become more difficult than she'd ever expected. But in order to make it work she knew there was only one answer.

An old woman picked up the phone, with a long, slow voice. This felt like the hardest call Sandy ever had to make.

"Hi, is Greta there please?"

"Just a minute. Can I say who this is?" She could hear a desperate sounding voice in the background say her name, and with the woman's intonation of "Sandy," there was new hope.

"Sandy! Is that you?"

"Yes, Greta. It's me!"

"I've been trying to call you for a half hour. Where are you?"

"I'm at the police station. You were trying to call me? Is everything okay?" Sandy couldn't believe she was asking this.

"I was so worried about you. And that creep told me you'd kidnapped Andy!" Sandy knew there wasn't a moment to lose.

"I need a restraining order. He hit me. Andy's here."

"Oh, my God! He said you went crazy and threw his records across the room, then knocked him over with an ottoman. He told me he'd be calling the police as soon as he got off the phone with me!"

"Quick, Greta. Tell the sergeant all about last night so I can get a restraining order first!" Sandy handed him the phone.

She hoped she hadn't said anything in front of him which could incriminate her in Kyle's so-called allegation. He'd looked at her for a moment like he wasn't sure who to believe.

"Yes, ma'am. That's right. You saw him attack 2.... With the baby on the table. Ms. Arthur had to run out of the kitchen to make sure.... I see. I see." Sandy felt more confident as he kept nodding. "All right, ma'am. We'll draw it right up and get it out to him." Yes!

"What's that? Oh, I don't know where she'll be staying tonight." This suddenly made Sandy remember what lay ahead.

"Here, Ms. Arthur." He gave her back the phone.

"Thanks, Greta. You don't know what a help you've been." She began to get a little emotional again.

"Where are you and Andy going to stay? At a hotel?"

"No. We don't get paid 'til Saturday. The shelter downtown."

"No way. I won't hear of it. You come right over here."

"Really? Oh, Greta, I'm so sorry about before at Sarno's."

"So am I. But never mind that now, we'll talk later. In the meantime, here's my address. Get here as soon as you can so we can figure out what we're going to do about all this." Greta gave Sandy her address, and she once again felt new hope.

While Kyle had been trying to convince his pals who seemed to feel at odds about getting involved in his domestic squabbles to act as hostile witnesses against Sandy before he called the police, they showed up at his door with the restraining order, and a warning about the noise and loud music.

When Sandy arrived at Greta's, the door was answered by an elderly woman who had the same light skin tones as Greta, only with whiter hair. "Hi, I'm Adrian. Greta's mother. Come in."

Greta appeared in the doorway leading to a flight of stairs at the back of the room. She looked so unusual in her bathrobe, because Sandy wasn't used to seeing her in anything but an apron.

She gave Sandy a hug and kissed Andy. "How are you doing, kiddo? I see you've met my mother. Mom, have you ever seen such a sweet little boy?"

"He sure is a handsome one. But I know you 2 have a lot to talk about so I'll just be getting to bed now." Sandy now felt sort of funny about being here, like a sudden imposition.

She noticed many pictures on the wall, most of them with familial traits. Seeing what looked like a much younger Adrian alongside a man who had to be Greta's father beside Greta's child portrait made Sandy remember the lack of love in her childhood. Beside it she saw 3 smug looking adolescent boys, one with dark blond hair like Greta's, with the other 2 darker with red hair and lots of freckles. She couldn't help notice how the darker ones resembled the man looking like Greta's father, and the lighter one looked like he could've been Greta's twin. "Nice looking family," said Sandy, trying to warm the environment more.

Greta was about to answer her when there was talking from the room Adrian had gone into. "Who that?"

"Sandy."

"Who?" continued the elderly male voice.

"Sandy," Adrian enunciated slowly for him. "She works with Greta at the restaurant. She's staying upstairs in Greta's apartment with her."

"Oh, Chandy. Oh."

"In case you're wondering that's my dad, Milton. He's had a stroke from too much womanizing." Sandy found this shocking, but laughed along with Greta to keep the tension light. "Of course, mom's obviously forgiven him, otherwise he'd be state property."

"Oh, Greta, I don't know what to say." What probably should have been some relief over another having troubles too only made Sandy sadder.

"What's there to say? We're both women with

scarred and troubled pasts. And speaking of scarred, he really got you there tonight, didn't he?" They were now at the base of the stairs from where a bright light above the door illuminated them.

"I mean look how this turned out," she continued, as Sandy followed her up the stairs. "He smacks you, so now you've got to go. The restraining order's supposed to keep you free of him. Instead, if you're lucky, and a lot of that depends on strategy, it might keep him free of you. In YOUR own home. That YOUR hard earned money goes to pay for. Go figure."

This didn't sound too promising, and Sandy wished the police had been called earlier so they could've been there at the very moment Sandy found Andy in the cellar. Then at least they'd definitely have him for child abuse.

"You know though, Greta, part of this is my fault too. If I hadn't let this go so long.."

"Sandy, shut up! Shut the fuck up, sit down, and let me tell you something." Sandy complied, knowing this was all for her own good. "It was my fault too. That my life went to hell in crap. That I'm living here in this isolated hovel, taking care of those 2 old fuckshits down there that made it all possible." Sandy had a hard time not cringing at this.

"But you see, Sandy, the point I'm trying to make here is that while you and ONLY you are your own worst enemy, you ALSO have the choice of being your own best friend as well. Do you sort of follow what I'm getting at?"

"Sort of." In spite of Greta's sardonic rambling, Sandy felt the warmth of a truly caring person.

Andy started to cry a little. "Oh, what's da matter, wittle one? Do you want Auntie Greta to hold you?" Greta gestured for Sandy to hand him to her and she did. In less than a minute he was cooing.

"You sure are wonderful with him."

"Look at the 3 of us," said Greta, pointing to their reflections in the mirror on the wall. "You and I are the oreo cookie, with Andy the glass of chocolate milk." They giggled.

"And if my little boy was here, there'd be regular milk too."

"You have a son?"

"Would have. If I'd left my scum ex-husband, Frank, before he beat me so hard when I was pregnant, that I miscarried."

This time Sandy couldn't help cringing. "Oh, my God!"

"And notice too, if you will. How there are no pictures of the family anywhere on MY wall." Sandy sensed Greta wanted to vent it all now, and she was more than okay to be there for her.

"But what about your ex? What happened to him?" She didn't want to seem too inquisitive, yet it was hard not to seek more information, in light of all this.

"Doing 10 to 15 in the state pen for man-slaughter. But I'm sure he'll be after me once he gets out. By then I plan to have the gun I should've owned 2 years ago. Then at least my son would be alive, even if I ended up in the can. Of course, if I'd made the right choice about men in the first place, I'd have REALLY been better off."

Sandy couldn't help but wonder how bad it would have been if she'd never given Kyle a chance. So she'd still be basically the doormat of that Southern bitch, but at least she'd always be set in her home life, and never on the run. And there was always that touch of elegance which certainly beat this scene.

"You know what, Greta? I really do miss the South. With all its style, those beautiful rivers, the jazz and bridges. And it's so much warmer. Why is it that because of a few bad people, nice people like us have to completely rearrange our lives?"

Greta shook her head and the empathy was obviously mutual.

"But you know what, Sandy? Maybe these last couple of nights have been a wakeup call for both of us. You know when I hollered at you at the restaurant, it was only because I didn't want to see you get hurt as badly as I did."

"I know that. Believe me, if you hadn't stuck your neck out to Mr. Johnson this morning on my behalf, I don't know where I'd be now." Sandy knew how dreadful that speculation was. "And I haven't even thanked you yet."

A tear rolled down her cheek, causing a twinge of pain from where Kyle had hit her. "Ouch!"

"Here, let me put a little warm water on that." Greta gave Andy back to her and went to the faucet.

"Thanks," said Sandy, as Greta handed her a doused towel. "For everything."

"Don't mention it. Want a cup of coffee or something?"

"Tell you what. How about letting me make the coffee. After all, you've already done everything else for me so far."

"So tell me more about your family," said Sandy, while she sipped. It seemed like familiarity would be the key to reaching out.

"Well, remember the 3 boys whose picture you saw on the wall downstairs? My brother and 2 cousins. Raped me when I was 9."

Sandy almost gagged on the coffee. This had to be the most bizarre night of her life. Whatever kind of bonding was available in times of trouble, she'd now begun to believe she really had the upper hand.

"Oh, I'm sorry. I guess this isn't a good time for a game of can you top this. But you did ask about my family."

"But what about your parents? Do they know?"

"Oh, yeah. Of course, it was MY fault. At least it was in Adrian's eyes. After all, I'd been exposing myself at the beach, what with being a little girl with nothing better to do than try to build sand castles while my sweet brother, Danny, and cousins Joe and Mike were wizzing on them. Hey, I mean they were exposing themselves too, right? Only thing is, they couldn't take the heat and they were stronger than me. And even though Milton was off somewhere laying one of his secretaries, I guess he thought it was okay too. After all, years later he put all 3 of them through law school. And although this practically ruined him financially, they're all very successful corporate attorneys in Manhattan. Yup. Hawes, McClaren and Hawes. Not a Jew in the bunch. Just incestuous rapists and sodomists."

"You know, I think the main reason for me going with Kyle was because he was black too." Sandy had wanted a subject change.

"Hey, listen. You don't have to sell me on the concept of solidarity. In fact, I'm even rather the forgiving kind. Why do you think I'm willing to stay here and take care of those 2. It sure ain't for a debt of gratitude."

"Well then I guess you're a better person than me. I hate everyone in my family, not to mention all those foster guardians I had. Before they abandoned me, me, my brothers and sisters went around playing minstrel shows, shining shoes and doing whatever odd jobs were necessary to get us spending money. We never got no allowance. Then with all that, you'd think all us kids would stay together for the long haul. But we were forced together by the state as children, fought like cats and dogs, stabbed each other in the back to try to get the approval of anyone who cared about us, when in fact, nobody really gave a rat's ass. I was always having to fend for myself, and the one up side was I learned to cook and clean, since in most of those places our caretakers never even did that. It's a wonder the state didn't disown them, let alone putting us in their care."

Sandy and Greta looked off into space for a moment and began to giggle.

"Here's to the funny tragedies of life," chimed Greta, with her coffee cup raised. Sandy clinked her own against it.

And so the sleeping arrangements were made. Sandy and Andy would get to use the little guest bedroom off the kitchenette. It was plushly carpeted so he could sleep in comfort on the floor with a blanket over him.

Perhaps tomorrow Sandy would send a courier to pick up some personal belongings from her house. In the meantime, all that mattered now was her and Andy's safety.

She found the bed very comfortable. Yet her sleep was filled with demonic dreams of sacrifice and Satan worship. In one of them, Madame H'Ouvre was gesturing to her and her siblings to enter a flaming pit one by one, while Ku Klux Klan members indicated who was next by pointing to them, each time another had gone in. Then she found herself being raped by Satan in a ceremony where hooded druids stood around them in a circle, bowing and chanting. When he finally revealed his face, to her horror she saw it was Kyle with horns and a tail. In the final dream she was all alone running as fast as she could across a barren desert as thunder crackled and lightning fired all around her. The sound of a baby crying was what she seemed to be after in the distance, and the sudden shrill noise of sirens going off woke her up.

Still groggy, she overheard some talk about insurance money. As she sat up, she realized it was Adrian addressing Milton at the foot of the stairs.

Sandy looked down at the floor. Andy had woken up and was a little cranky. But it was still the middle of the night, and she couldn't understand why the sirens were going off, or why Greta's parents had been up.

"Greta," she called, after picking Andy up and peeking out the bedroom door. "Oh, my God!" 2 police officers stood over Greta. She lay there on the floor, with her eyes and mouth wide open. Her pupils were dilated. As awful as those dreams were, Sandy prayed to herself this was another one.

"Sandra Arthur?" said the junior patrolman. "I'm so sorry." Sandy couldn't believe what was happening. She felt so numb with grief she staggered backwards before he caught her. He nodded to his partner who covered Greta with a white sheet.

"We got the guy who did this out in the car,"

he said.

"Name's Kyle Samuelson. We figure he broke in about 20 minutes ago. Strangled her. I guess the motive was robbery. It usually is in a case like this."

"Do you want to come downtown with us now and answer a few questions?" said the other one. "You don't have to, but it might help clear up a few things." Sandy cried as hard as ever. She never went with them. When she finally left to go home, Sandy ignored Adrian and Milton on the way out.

It was so shocking how all they could care about was Greta's insurance settlement. All Greta had cared about was keeping Andy from that monster's clutches, and it'd cost her her life.

At the funeral, Sandy felt like she may have been the only one with the right to be there. She spoke to no one other than to say the last rites along with the minister during the service. She tried not to look at anyone either, other than to give long glaring glances across the aisle at Greta's smug looking brother and cousins in their spit-shined suits, no doubt there for the prime purpose of seeking what if any booty they might obtain from her settlement. She also shot a glare at Mr. Johnson, who was prepared to let her go from Sarno's for something that was hardly her fault.

But since Sandy had now decided to take Andy, return to New Orleans, and check her P.O. box for any responses she may have received on her résumé before she took off with that creep, it was pretty certain she'd never have to see any of them again.

The one thing she'd do differently this time would be to buy the gun Greta should've had in her apartment 3 nights earlier. In case anyone wanted to take her down now, they'd be going right down with her.

After the gun was purchased, Sandy loaded it, packed up her car and got ready to roll. She felt pangs of annoyance as Andy began whining a little.

"Don't you ever think of turning on me," she muttered, clasping her hands to the base of the gun. "You're the main reason for this whole situation. And I'd just as soon blow you away as I would anyone else who'd stab me in the back. You got it?" His noises softened slightly, as he looked up at her in his infantile innocence. She nodded self-righteously, and they were off.

Her life about to begin anew, Sandy shot down the road toward the site of her roots, readier than ever to grab any bull by the horns and squash it.

The Ghost
of the Widower

B enny lay back in his lazy boy recliner, lit a cigarette, and gazed up at the glowing zodiac chart on the wall. If he held the butt straight out, and blew a smoke ring, he could pick the most prosperous sign of the day by seeing which one it was nearest to when it vanished.

Lorna had taught him this, along with most of her eccentric practices. Yet it was this quaint habit of hers, he'd discovered before the others, which had first attracted him to her. That and the way she often fluttered her deep, dark eyelashes, enhanced exquisitely by the multi-colored rouges and lipsticks she knew how to apply so provocatively.

The room was filled with remnants of her. All the medieval charms and talismans she'd collected in her quest for becoming the all-knowing philosophical queen, glowed and sparkled in the dark like friendly spirits. It was as if she'd commanded them to watch over him, and see to it he never lost sight of their magnificent purpose, in order to help him carry on.

But there was nothing special about his grief— it continued to manifest itself in spite of all her precious artifacts and memories—as if to say, hey, I'm JUST as real. And from it he was supposed to build strength and hope, based on Lorna's belief adversity was a 2-way mirror one could look at both ways.

They'd made all the plans for a great life together—the big old-fashioned wedding with lots of decor, music and guests. Of course, their own lives had been so different that any semblance of organization between their families and friends would've been a miracle in and of itself. But theirs was a love of challenges which made it all the more special. Benny with his clean cut pals from the service who'd done their nation proud in battle during some of the more recent showings of U.S. imperialism. Lorna with her dozen Gypsy siblings who danced their way into his life at a family gathering of hers he'd gone to in an attempt to make himself one with her people. Of course, there was some adversity on the parts of certain senior members of both clans, and also of Benny's sister, Julia, who felt Benny was throwing his life away on someone who was way too outrageous to be her sister-in-law.

But as Benny had noted, for the first time in his life — he'd been really happy — because before he met her, his life had been a simple, straight and narrow routine of expected performance and production. Now there'd be personal satisfaction which came with being one's own man — something he'd been taught philosophically in Sunday school, through little league baseball, then later on, during high school and college activities of an extracurricular nature, and the service; but he'd never really lived for himself.

And it hadn't taken him long to discover Lorna felt the same way about her own life. But with her, the pressures of being part of a nomadic group in the late 20th century created even more of a bond with him. His desire to see the world, which was part of his reason for joining the military, had led him to convince her to settle down, after they'd both shared the restless experience of travel fatigue.

The night they'd met near the base, Benny's sergeant showed his grim sense of humor by suggesting to the squad they find out whether they'd die in battle by visiting the Gypsy tent on the outskirts of camp, and having their fortunes told.

Benny only did it on a dare from a fellow cadet, who told him he'd cover his latrine duty, if he'd be so bold.

But when he entered the tent, he saw his fortune right there. Lorna was blowing a smoke ring at the zodiac chart. "Shhh," she told him. "The stars are all at rest. And it must be very quiet, otherwise my reading will be false." He couldn't believe what he was seeing. It was like she was a high school kid, experimenting with a new fad. Her jewelry chimed as she stood up and pointed. "Pisces! That's the most prosperous sign of the day."

"That's amazing," he said with sincere fascination. "I'm a Pisces!" It was so perfect—the timing, the moment—just right.

Then their eyes met for the first time. There was no mistaking the feelings that passed between them—the stark but complicated sensation of mutual rescue from a void in their lives, neither had realized they'd been cursed with until now.

"Would you like me to read your fortune, good soldier?" She'd asked this with a slightly upturned smile, indicative of a strong friendship seemed meant to be.

"MY fortune? I'm not sure I really believe in them." Benny had surprised himself with this revelation, as his intent had been to try to get her to show him how it was done. But at the moment, he felt so confused about what was happening — like he couldn't understand how to act, or come across, because he'd never really experienced anything like it before.

She giggled and shook her head slightly, perhaps as if to say she'd shun any other skeptic, but since it was him, it was okay. And Benny now felt relief at her reaction, realizing how lucky he was he hadn't offended or upset her.

"So maybe you just wanted to find out more about Gypsies?" He never knew how fascinating they could be. It was as if he'd opened the door to a familiar old closet and found himself in a palace. But what did it mean — why was it happening to him? To a man who'd always felt somewhat aloof of others, it seemed eerie.

As it had turned out, the rest of her clan was at a festival on the Rhine, while she'd stayed behind with a sense of urgency. Apparently, she was considered the most rebellious — yet also the most clairvoyant of the group — and after explaining this to him, their shared revelation was delightful.

"You mean you stood your family up tonight, because you knew I'd be here?" For the first time since he'd joined the service, Benny actually wished everyone he left back home could see him.

"Yes. You're the stranger I dreamed about. But why are you so surprised? I take my dream herbs every night before I go to sleep. After I spend all day brewing them." Dream herbs. What a concept. Definitely too weird to provide the rest of the world with just yet. On the other hand, what a profit could be made.

"I'm sorry. It's just that I've never heard of those. But who cares? They obviously work. And I'm not sorry about that. By the way, I'm...." He started to put his hand out.

"Vinnie, right? You're Vinnie." Not exactly right, but close enough to almost shock him. Very similar phonetics and the same number of syllables.

"Benny! But hey, that was awfully close. You're amazing! And what might your name be?" She lowered her head momentarily, and it suddenly occurred to Benny she might be sad about being wrong.

But then she turned around, picked up a violin, and began to play and sing what sounded like a Gypsy folk song which could've been written just for her.

"I'm Lorna, princess of the Gypsies, and I love to sing and dance. I'm Lorna, princess of my family, my specialty is romance. Come on, Benny, dance with me, now. This is a special occasion! I'm Lorna, and I'll make your heart sing; I'm Lorna, I blow the smoke ring, I'm Lorna, princess of the Gypsies, and why won't you dance with ME!"

Benny felt slightly foolish for a moment, yet he loved the experience he was having, and didn't want to lose it. So he began to dance right along with her, hoping neither anyone from the base might pass by, hear the noise, and come into the tent, or any member of her clan might do the same. But the more he kept it up, the less inhibited he felt, and finally, Benny felt he hadn't a care in the world.

"Well, Lorna. I take it this isn't how you treat all your visitors," he said, when they'd finally stopped, after going for a good 5 minutes. "It is Lorna, right?" he added, most jokingly.

Now she laughed as hard as ever, put down the violin, and gave him the biggest hug he ever had. "Oh, Benny. How would you like to join the Gypsies, eh?" she finally said, after composing.

Could she have been serious? This was the most incredibly bittersweet night of his life. The choice of possibly falling in love, or putting his life on the line for his country stared him squarely in the face. And the only way he could achieve the former at this point would be to go AWOL.

"Lorna, we just met. And in 2 weeks I ship out to guard a very important U.S. interest." She gave him a long, passionate kiss on the cheek. At least she hadn't given up on them. Or maybe this was just her way of wishing him luck.

"Well then, Mister Benny, good soldier. There's

nothing like an authentic Gypsy token to guard you against all danger. Here." Lorna removed what looked like a small, gold-plated chalice from the pocket of her robe and handed it to him. "Now I know you'll come through safe and sound. And we can dance together all over again."

Without question, Benny now felt a new confidence about his chances for survival. Although it seemed somewhat absurd, he was able to appreciate the fact there was much in the world which was unexplainable—especially for those who just spent their whole lives simply accepting the inevitable—without bothering to try to find out more. From here on, he'd never again be like that.

"You're sure quite a musician, Lorna. Are you self-taught?"

It suddenly occurred to Benny he hadn't thanked her for the chalice. "Oh, thank you," they both said, simultaneously.

"This is amazing," he continued, feeling more and more like he'd been blessed by some deity, but also wondering if perhaps his mind was playing tricks on him.

"Amazing?" Lorna asked. "Benny, you need to learn we're all at one with each other." She proceeded to unveil a diagram of shapes and lines which was under a canvas Benny had thought might have been a painting she'd been working on. "Look here. This is our world at the center. And these are the astral planes you and I are on." She pointed to 2 circles which appeared concurrent and right above the middle of the chart. "I've spent my whole life researching this. The key is learning to tell the positions linked closest together. That way I know whose destinies interact the most. Of course, everything with a soul has a place here, but the astral planes you and I are on are so close, our destinies are almost one."

Benny was totally spooked, but never more content. Of course, this stuff was way too complicated for him to try to learn in one night. Yet he believed it was his fate to do so soon.

"Well that's great, Lorna. But you still haven't told me...."

"Simple. My astral plane is innovation. It includes music." She went on to explain how his astral plane was enhancement, which went hand in hand with innovation, and was just about central to it. And since both astral planes were so close to the center of the universe, those whose souls who were that close were inherently connected.

And after giving him much about Gypsy lore and legend, Lorna invited him to a gathering of her clan which would take place in her tent just before he was scheduled to move out, and also just before she and her clan would be moving on to another temporary location around the countryside—which was always celebrated by a big festival the night before the Gypsies' departure.

Suffice it to say, the next couple of weeks for

Benny were quite involved. Writing letters back home, describing Lorna to everyone in his life, as well as visiting her in the tent, as often as he could. Unfortunately, he felt some dissonance with Lorna's big, mustachioed father and uncles, who'd picked up his intentions to take their baby away. But on the night of their festival, Lorna's mother announced to them they'd planned to wed in the United States, after Benny had finished serving his country, and being she was most influential—primarily with her dominance of men—the point was reached where they had to give them their blessing, and commit to flying over for the affair.

Just about everyone in Benny's family had been opposed to it, save for a few young cousins who figured a shindig like that'd be a great opportunity for them to horse around and pig out on the wedding cake.

And they might've completely rejected the idea, were it not for the fact that when Benny finally got to serve his country, he managed to survive a gun battle with a tough warlord, rendering him heroic in the eyes of his government and everyone who knew him. Which meant Uncle Sam was willing to pay for not only the wedding, but the flight of the Gypsies back and forth to and from the U.S. Yet before he had the chance to be decorated, Benny found to his shock and horror, the chalice Lorna had given him was disfigured by the bullet lodged in it meant for him.

"Everything in our universe happens for a reason," Lorna had told him. "And nothing can occur without creating some kind of a mutual disturbance. But nothing can ever end, it can only lead to another beginning, designed to remind us to grow, learn and feel enlightened by the knowledge that adversity is a 2-way mirror one could look at both ways."

These were the only words of comfort Benny had to fall back on, after Lorna's sudden fatal brain aneurysm on the plane ride with him, his fellow cadets and her family back to his home town.

And so instead of a wedding, all the people in Benny's and Lorna's lives had to celebrate a memorial service together. And after it was over, Lorna's remains were flown back home with her people, while Benny had kept all her stuff at their insistence, so he could always feel a part of her was still with him.

Now as he sat back in his darkened living room, his sister, Julia paid him a visit. "Come on, Benny. You've been staying here in the dark, pretending for 6 months now. You need to get on with your life already."

He took a deep breath, knowing she was right, but not about to admit it without some kind of blow up. After all, it wasn't the kind of thing one just did casually. "Hey, sis. You know what? Why don't you go back home to mom and dad. With your perfect little lives, and your set schedules, and leave me the fuck alone. You think I need you coming over and telling me I'm stuck in sorrow? Here, you want to see what I think of your damn advice?" Benny jumped up, grabbed Lorna's violin and threw it in the lit fireplace. "There!" Then he took her tarot cards and did the same. Then her dream herbs, palm reading kit, zodiac and astral plane chart. "There! You happy? I'm letting go!" He began sobbing ferociously while Julia hugged him. And through the flames' warmth, Benny finally felt her soul forgive his guilt.